It's A Dirty Rotten Shame

Kaz Clark

Published by Kaz Clark
Publishing partner: Paragon Publishing, Rothersthorpe
First published 2022

ISBN 978-1-78222-961-2

Book design, layout and production management by Into Print
www.intoprint.net
+44 (0)1604 832149

To my children, love always x

1

My name is Ruby. I was born in a hurry on Bonfire night. According to my mother, I didn't even have the decency to wait till she made it to the bedroom. Instead, I arrived lifeless upon the kitchen table to the scream of rockets disturbing the heavens. In attendance was my father and Vodka Vera, who practically lived at our house when she wasn't on a bender. For once she decided to cut the drinking short. It was my first lucky break. She knew exactly what to do with a silent baby, had me filling my lungs with fresh air in no time. Obviously I'm very grateful. Trouble was she made sure I never forgot it.

As I grew to be a nosy little tyke, I soon acquired the talent for earwigging, which was just as well, and I'll tell you why. My kith and kin were over-fond of secrets. Listening in to the gaggle of gossipers supping tea in our kitchen, I learned things a kid should never learn.

Then the only Uncle I had went and got himself dead. That's when I recalled a previous ear-wigging incident. I remembered 'cos it sure as hellfire scared the living daylights out of me.

It was New Years Eve. I was nine. Swags of dusty paper chains stretched across the ceiling. A Christmas tree stood tired and twinkling in the corner of the living-room. In the shade of its lower branches fallen pine needles littered the floor, burrowed into socks if you were foolish enough to go slipper-less. Smells of mince pies mingled with cheap market perfume. Dad softly tickled the ivories on the old upright piano. Mum played at hostess. The place heaved at the seams with friends and neighbours, or anyone else who happened to be passing by. Good job too, seeing as the Blackbee clan sorely lacked numbers with just the five of us left in the universe.

Uncle Stavros drove down from the Smoke in his black Humber with tan leather seats.

Granny Bee sat in the back like royalty, dressed fit for mourning, a face over stacked with wrinkles. I wasn't keen on her. Needless to say, the feeling was mutual.

In contrast, Uncle Stavros preferred well-cut suits, jazzy ties, and gold cufflinks to match his gold front tooth. When he took his porkpie hat off, his Brylcreemed hair shone like a polished conker. In my opinion he was only an average looker, but women practically swooned at his winkle pickers. Without fail Vera flirted outrageously with him, her flapping eyelashes almost whipping up a draught. Without fail he passed her a half bottle of Smirnoff. She slipped it into her handbag as smooth as a seasoned shoplifter.

"Oh Stavros, if I was ten years younger I'd show you a thing or two." She giggled like a dizzy teenager.

I heard him laugh that laugh of his that shook all the common sense out of women who ought to know better.

"I bet you would, me darlin'," he said, "and I'd have let you."

I saw him pat her skinny backside. So did Mum. She narrowed her hazel eyes, curved her coral painted lips into a sneer.

"Mickey," she said, "that brother of yours could charm the knickers of a nun."

"Yep, reckon he could an' all, Joan, given half the chance," Dad said.

"Well, have a word with him. He's not on some backstreet in Soho now, is he?"

I caught Dad give Mum a shifty sideways look. Sometimes, even at that young age, I got the impression Uncle Stavros rubbed her up the wrong way, which was odd 'cos all the ladies loved him. And so did I, even though he sang Sinatra songs when over the limit on liquor. Who'd have thought the biggest secret in my family's closet concerned him, of all people.

"It's where I come from, Joan, the backstreets of Soho," Dad said.

With just my lugholes flapping, I kept the rest of me as still possible, waited for Mum's reply. She fussed with the sleeve of her bronze coloured dress. She'd sewed it special on the old Singer for the end of year shindig. I took a second to admire her handiwork. She was real nifty with a needle, a skill I much appreciated as a teenager. In fact, she had a nice sideline going at one time knocking out copies of Mary Quant numbers. Our house was often awash with nearly naked females having a fitting.

"But we're here now, Mickey, aren't we?" Mum laid her right cheek atop his head.

Her eyes slid west towards Uncle Stavros. "I just don't want it spoiled by the past."

I don't mind admitting a bit of worry settled in my belly when I heard that. After all, we were fine on our estate, a spit throw from the south coast, weren't we? Dad worked at the dockyard, my best friend, Grace Doyle with the polio leg, lived next door. Practically everyone had a dodgy deal or two running to make ends meet, and that included the painted Marjory Watkins. She lived at number twenty-two with no husband, kept body and soul together working evenings in the entertainment business, if you know what I mean. Life was perfectly safe if you stuck to the unwritten rules, the main rule being don't crap on your own garden path, unless you were prepared to pay the consequences. A few paid. Not many made the same mistake twice.

Anyway, I felt the worry waltz around faster. That's the problem with earwigging, isn't it, you don't always get the full story. Fortunately, Dad decided the moment had come to liven up the party. His fingers crashed upon the piano keys, startled Mum. Her lips scrolled over teeth. I saw a lipstick stain on the left incisor. She laughed. It sounded a shade wild.

"You fool, Mickey." She took a swing, jabbed him gently on the chin, moved off to mingle with the guests. Her dress rustled as she brushed past me.

A grin split my face. I knew what was coming. Dad stood, scraped the stool sideways with a foot, spread his arms wide, flexed his fingers. Someone cheered. Then he sang that his nerves were shaken and his brain rattled. The party had started.

The earwigging incident that sure as hellfire scared the living daylights out of me, happened late in the evening. I was full to overflowing on fizzy and high jinxes when I began to flag. Slumping alongside Vera, as usual three sheets to the wind gone on vodka, I yawned wide, snuggled my face into her bony midriff. Kids do that. One minute we're bombing around like noisy brats, the next we're asleep on our feet.

"Come on, sweet pea," Mum said. "It's way past your beddy-byes. Give Daddy a kiss goodnight and I'll tuck you up."

Well, I knew where to find Dad. Just minutes ago I'd heard Uncle Stavros say, "Let's go outside for a puff, Mickey."

So that's where they'd be, in the garden, sucking on Havana cigars Uncle had plucked from his jacket pocket. Dragging my tired body to the kitchen I spied them through the open door. As they puffed on the fat cigars the ends burned red as glowing embers. Whorls of smoke escaped their mouths into the crisp night air. The moon sat low in a star dusty sky; a cold breeze jingled the plastic coated clothesline against its poles. I toddled a bit closer, waited for a lull in the conversation. I wasn't allowed to interrupt grown-ups talk. Mum was strict on good manners, said they never cost anyone a brass farthing. That day I wished I had interrupted before Uncle said, "Black Jack's been asking after you, Mickey."

"Has he now," Dad said.

"Yeah, he's not happy about something, wants you to pay a visit."

"I'll be up at the end of the month as usual, Stavros. What's going on?"

"Nothing's going on. Why do you always think there is?" Uncle sounded sulky, like me with a touch of the others.

"Could it be something to do with your track record?" Dad's voice was edged with scorn.

"Give it a rest, Mickey. I made one mistake; it's not the end of the world. But that Jack, off his bleeding rocker, he is, the crazy son of a b...," and he used the word Mum once called the flighty little strumpet from number ten. "Needs locking up before some poor sod gets murdered, he does."

Well, I'm not ashamed to say I screamed. It was the kind of scream that curls the toes, bristles the fine hairs on the back of the neck. Before I could draw breath to let rip another, Dad's hands gripped my shoulders, shook me till my teeth chattered in my mouth. Then his arms trapped me in a bear hug. I heard shushing noises rumble in his chest.

Problem was I couldn't make myself shush even if I'd tried my hardest. Once the heebie-jeebies gets a stranglehold all hope of shushing flies out the window, doesn't it. The only thing I managed right then was to cry. With my kisser pressed into the roughness of his donkey jacket, I let the tears roll.

"What in heaven's name is happening out here?" Mum wrestled me off Dad. I wrapped my limbs tight around her like a drowning man would a piece of driftwood.

"Nothing," Dad said. "I didn't even know she was here 'til she started bellowing."

"So she's bellowing for nothing, is she?" Mum snorted, pressed her lips to my hot brow, threw a look full of daggers at Uncle Stavros.

"Look, Joan, we were having a puff and talking, that's all."

"You and bloody Stavros," Mum snarled, "I swear I'll swing for the pair of you if there's any trouble brewing, Mickey Blackbee, you mark my words."

With that parting shot she marched inside, slammed the door, set me on my feet. I milked the upset for a while longer, grizzled my best grizzle as a clean tea towel was wiped over my face. Vera swayed into the kitchen, said, "What's wrong with her?"

"I don't know," Mum said. "Mickey says him and Stavros were only talking when she started kicking up a rumpus."

I watched Vera tap out a Woodbine. She watched me watching her, narrowed one eye as she flared up a match, lit the choker. She dragged in, blew out slowly, said, "I see, no doubt earwigging again. She's a bugger for that, Joan, isn't she?"

I treated her to a glare. She kept a glare on me as she carefully lowered herself onto a chair. I attempted another grizzle. It sounded like a cat in dire straits.

"Well, whatever she heard upset her, my poor sweet pea." Mum hugged me to her ample bosom, rocked me east then west.

"Poor sweet pea? My arse is she. You never hear anything good earwigging. The sooner she learns that the better. Overtired is her problem, Joan. You know she's a misery when she's overtired, should have been in bed hours ago."

"And that's where she's going now. Put the whistler on, Vera, I could do with a nice strong cuppa." She led me by the hand up the stairs, tucked me into bed, left the landing light blazing 'cos the dark and I weren't the best of buddies. But sometime during that hour just before dawn, when the night terrors do the most damage, I woke with Black Jack on my mind, scrambled to my parents bed, crawled in between them.

"There's a nasty man, Mummy," I whimpered.

"No there isn't, sweet pea, there's no nasty man here." She cuddled me close into her warm body that smelled of sleep and Ponds cold cream.

And I wanted to believe her, only I knew what I had earwigged. I also knew I shouldn't blab about it. After all, just 'cos I was nine didn't mean I was stupid, did it?

So I kept it stored as a memory, which proved mighty handy six years later. Black Jack came a calling, and he didn't travel down alone. He brought a gun for company.

2

*I*t was the day of the dead crow. That's how I knew there was a tragedy on the horizon. I had just turned fifteen, was suffering from a bad case of infatuation for Denny Doyle, Grace's oldest brother. I'd been suffering for some time, way before the midnight deliveries, when only tom cats should be out on the prowl, stopped happening. I was never a hundred per cent sure who brought the crates of booze, the boxes of tinned goods, but I was pretty certain Uncle Stavros had something to do with it, 'cos Mum often said, "That brother of yours has his finger in too many pies, Mickey, he'll get burned one of these days, then you'll be sorry."

I guess Dad must have listened for once. They took to shooting off to London in the Hillman Minx, on the excuse of visiting Granny Bee. On their return the car was jam packed with contraband, a roll or two of material for Mum's dressmaking venture. It wasn't too hard to figure out the visits weren't just for duty.

Of course, in hindsight, I realise my parents were bootleggers. That suited me just fine. I stayed over at Grace's; saw more of Denny, who was too handsome by far and knew it. He was pushing nineteen, mad on Elvis, kept his dark curly hair too long to be decent, had the makings of a rocker nicely developing. During the day, he worked as an apprentice chippie. At other times he stripped lead and copper piping from derelict buildings, which he sold at the scrap yard for cash in hand, no questions asked.

Or his surly mates would slouch, hunchbacked, knuckles almost grazing the ground, over the scrubby patch of lawn like urban gorillas to fiddle about with a Triumph Tiger Cub. It stood against the fence in various states of disrepair, leaking oil, refusing to be kick-started. Sometimes Mr Doyle, a wiry, black eyed Irishman, took pity on his eldest, fiddled with the Triumph too. Sometimes, when the frustrations hit a high, spanners sailed through the air, and he'd shout, "Fecking heap of shite."

I liked Mr Doyle. Word was he had Latin blood flowing through his veins owing to a shipwreck decades ago. Apparently, only a handful of Spanish sailors made it safe to the shores of Ireland, the rest ended up in Davy Jones' locker. Word was he had visions. You know what I mean, don't you? Mr Doyle saw the deceased, had conversations with them, especially after downing a gallon of Guinness with a whiskey top. Most folk thought it was the drink talking, but I thought there was something to it, 'cos at the fated party, I overheard a message he received from the other side. Turned out there was truth in what the spirits told him.

Anyhow, Denny never paid me the kind of attention I desired. Grace said he was too busy sowing his wild oats. I reckoned once he'd finished sowing I'd be old enough, he'd be serious enough, it'll be happy ever after. I reckoned wrong. Denny Doyle put the kiss of death on me.

So, let's get back to the dead crow. The day was cursed the moment Vera came crashing through the kitchen door.

"Joan, oh my God, there's a crow on your garden path. It's as dead as a bloody doornail, an' all." She swayed. Her left hand grabbed hold of the butler sink, her right made the sign of the cross, the way a man of the cloth does. "Oh Joan, you know what that means, don't you?"

"Yes, Vera, I know what it means, according to you, that is."

I circled my peepers in their sockets, waited to hear the meaning of a dead crow.

Obviously it would be another of Vera's superstitions. She was full of them. This time, though, the information wasn't forthcoming. I tipped my chin east, pasted a look of encouragement on my kisser. The state of her caused my eyebrows to kiss above the bridge of my hooter. I noticed her complexion was as white as the underbelly of a cod on the fishmongers slab. It's usually flushed by a vodka breakfast. Come evening, there's a rosy hue. If you weren't familiar with her habits, you'd be fooled into thinking she was healthy.

"I don't know what a dead crow means, Vera," I said.

"It's an omen," she said.

"Just calm down," Mum said. "Put the wood in the hole, it's blowing a hooley out there."

Vera closed the door quietly, turned, opened wide her Rimmel red mouth, let rip a scream that could curdle milk. I watched her tonsils wobble, flinched in horror. Mum launched herself across the kitchen, reached her in two long strides, planted a slap on both sides of her face. The slapping had the desired effect. It stunned the scream into silence.

"Pull yourself together, Vera Williams," Mum hissed. "Bloody hell, you nearly gave me a heart attack."

The twin doors of the serving hatch burst open. Dad's head appeared, eyebrows that high his forehead resembled a sheet of corrugated iron.

"What the devils going on?" he said.

"Nothing's going on, Mickey." Mum smoothed palms down her pinny. "Now then, let's get a brew going, shall we?"

"There's a dead crow on our garden path." I ignored the hostile glare Mum threw my way, smiled a smile as smug as a cat with a mouthful of feathers.

"It's an omen," Vera said.

Dad snorted. "It's a bleeding old wives' tale, that's what it is."

I watched Mum strike a match, touch it to the gas ring on the cooker. A circle of yellow flames leapt to life. She banged the whistler upon them. The flames spread out, changed to blue. She gave Dad a nod. "Get rid of it, will you, Mickey."

"Bury it." Vera moved to the table, lowered herself onto a chair, pulled a silver hip flask from her handbag She unscrewed the top, helped herself to a generous slug.

"I'll say a little prayer for it, shall I?" Dad said.

I detected a tone of sarcasm in his voice, joined Vera at the table, treated her to one of my best smirks. It was wasted on her; she was busy glugging another slug.

"Well, it certainly wouldn't hurt to," she said. "Bury it, Mickey, and make sure it's buried deep."

"Bloody Nora, want it sprinkled with holy water as well?"

"Just do it," Mum said. "Just bury it deep, before she starts with the screaming abdabs again."

Dad sighed. His head disappeared back through the hatch. For a while we listened to him grumbling. Then we watched him pass through the kitchen, a pained expression on his face. I was torn between joining him for the burial, or staying put in hope of an earwig. Mum made the decision for me.

"Get that bread buttered, Ruby, we've a feast to rustle up. And don't you say a word about that ruddy crow, young lady, else you'll be for the high jump, you will."

I helped rustle up a feast instead of witnessing the last rites of a crow. A couple of tins of bully beef were fetched from the stockpile in the cupboard under the stairs, a jar of Branstons pickle. A dozen eggs were scrambled over a low heat, left to cool on the windowsill. The tea and talk brigade began to bring their contributions. Marjory Watkins cradled a sherry drenched trifle in her arms. Connie Doyle balanced a tray of bite size sausage rolls on the flat of her palm. I moved on from buttering bread to stabbing squares of cheese and pineapple together with wooden cocktail sticks. Vera took a knife to a hunk of boiled bacon, shaved off thin slices, arranged them on a plate. Old Ma Flowers wheezed in, a bottle of Cockburn's rubbing alongside a home baked Dundee cake.

"This'll get us in the swing of things." Her fag croaky voice paused to throw out a cough. "Then I'll tell you all about my first husband."

"Oh lovely, get the glasses, Vera," Mum said. "Only the proper port ones, mind."

"There's hardly a mouthful in those piddly little things," Vera said.

"That's because port should be sipped. Let's at least be civilised whilst we crucify Ma's first husband."

Pretty soon the bottle was empty except for the fumes. Pretty soon lips were flapping on a favourite subject. Men. I can assure you this pleased me no end. Just lately I'd been thinking quite a lot about kissing. In particular, was it true it could take you to heaven and back. That's what Maureen from the Co-op said. I reckoned she ought to know a thing or two 'cos she was courting Billy, the tattooed lorry driver. I also reckoned she could do better than that dimwit, though there's no accounting for taste, is there?

Nevertheless, I spent a splendid hour earwigging. And Old Ma Flowers didn't disappoint, either. I heard all there was to hear concerning the first husband who couldn't do the business.

"Is that really the God's honest, Ma?" Connie said.

"I'll swear it on the Bible if you want, ladies. He couldn't even raise a smile. Don't imagine your young whippersnapper Denny has trouble in that department, Connie. See he's got a new dolly bird hanging round his neck. Pretty little thing she is too."

"Bet she don't know what she's letting herself in for," Vera said, "poor cow."

My belly rolled a double somersault, my ticker banged against my ribcage. I sidestepped to the walk-in larder lest anyone else picked up the sound of it knocking on bone. So Denny Doyle had a new dolly bird, was obviously still hell bent on sowing his wild oats. I wondered how long I'd wait before he got to me, wondered if I should invest in a bit of practice with other boys. After all, I near enough knew all there was to know of the theory. Rosemary Collins had lifted a copy of the Kama Sutra from the library. She shared it with the click of girls I belonged to behind the bike shed at break, 'til it went missing in a locker raid.

Maybe more experience would show him I wasn't just the girl next door. Maybe then I'd be one of his poor cows.

"Well, a broken heart won't kill you," Mum said.

If I hadn't been secretly holed up in the larder I might have been tempted to dispute that fact. I mean, weren't I the expert on broken hearts? Didn't every new girl Denny hit on break another little piece of my heart. Luckily, Vera was on the same wavelength as me.

"It damn well can," she said. "A broken heart kills slowly, and each second is pure agony."

From my position in the larder I saw Mum's hand rest on Vera's right shoulder, give it a squeeze. I chanced a peep around the door, noticed faces now glowing with port and something else. I recognised the something else immediately. It was an extra shot of pity, like Grace gives me when I'm mooning over her brother.

"Steady on, my friend." Mum's tone was choked with compassion. "We're not on about your kind of broken heart."

Naturally, on hearing that, my curiosity was on red alert. What kind of broken heart did Vera have? What other kind was there? Instinct warned me another secret was ready to hit the light of day, a secret I wasn't sure I could handle. But my tootsies didn't so much as shuffle on the cool red quarry tiles, my lugholes stayed finely tuned. That's the trouble with me, I'm a sucker for a sob story. I've listened to many true-life tales, from the POW Steven Shaw, our neighbour on the left, from Dad on the waste of war, the innocent folk bombed to buggery in their own homes. Yet I knew sweet Fanny Adams about Vera, though she knew all the ins and outs about me. That's why I kept my breathing as shallow as I dared, waited, waited longer. The silence grew loud with the sound of buzzing in my brain. Any moment soon I'd collapse through lack of oxygen.

"Actually, I'm not working tonight. It'll be nice to see the New Year in with you lot for a change," Marjory said.

I gulped in air as Mum appeared in the larder doorway. She gave me a stern look, lips pressed tight together. I offered her a smile. In return she gave me the thumb sign to scarper, picked up a tray of spicy smelling mince pies, followed me out. I parked myself at the butler sink, felt the heat of five pairs of peepers burning holes in my back. I studied the leaf free lilac tree at the bottom of the garden. The branches were dusted with frost. Come summer it would miraculously burst into foliage and flower, its scent enticing bees and butterflies to busy themselves on the nectar.

"Not working, Marjory?" Old Ma said. "That's a turn-up for the books, isn't it?"

"Thought New Year was one of your best earners," Connie said.

"It is, but there's this man ..."

I turned my face west, watched a pink tinge make its way through the slap spread across Marjory's dial.

"There's always a man to ruin things," Vera sighed.

"This one's different."

"Different?" Mum said. "Well I never, Marjory Watkins. You've not once called a man different. Is it serious?"

"I think I'd like it to be. Oh I don't know. It probably won't last, considering."

"How long have you known him?" Old Ma said.

"Two months, three weeks and five days." Marjory laughed. "Not that I'm counting, of course. His name's Sid, he's from Pompey. He ferries top nobs around in his Roller and runs a used car business as well."

At that point my attention took a hike. I didn't care for the gossip on Second-hand Sid, was still hung up on broken hearts. As unlikely as it seemed, Vera and me had something in common. Denny Doyle was the cause of my broken heart. When I discovered the cause of hers, I wished I hadn't bothered. But first there was the party to get through, the dolly bird to size up, the Hokey-Cokey, Auld Lang Syne. And my initiation into Russian roulette.

3

*A*ll evening I dilly-dallied from room to room, eventually settled in the lounge. The party was resting in preparation for the big push at midnight. Conversation turned low, folk socialised in small groups. Men relived the triumph of the World Cup against Germany. Women discussed other women. Even Granny Bee and Steven Shaw found each other company, probably 'cos they were both a couple of fruit and nut cases. I was on my lonesome due to Grace getting cosy with her first ever beau. We'd once sworn on an ill gained quart of Woodpeckers never to let any boy ruin our friendship. Seemed to me she had every intention of allowing JJ Duffy to canoodle his way between us. I mentioned as much to her.

"Things aren't the same since you've taken up with Duffy," I said.

"What do you mean?" Grace said. "We still hang with the same old gang, don't we?"

"Yeah, but every time I turn around, there he is, like some lovesick puppy, that's what I mean. It's really pathetic, all that drooling and what have you."

"Are you jealous of my boyfriend, Ruby?" She had a concerned look on her kisser.

"Do me a favour." I sniffed, treated her to an Elvis lip curl. "I'm just saying, I wouldn't ditch my best friend for some stupid boy, would I?"

"Well, that's a fib if ever there was one. I'd be long gone if my brother gave you the glad eye, and don't you try denying it, either."

So I didn't, 'cos she was right. I'd ditch her without thinking twice if Denny gave me the glad eye, though if past experience was anything to go by, it was highly unlikely to come about. I was obviously destined for spinsterhood like Miss Martin, the postmistress, whose fiancée was shot down in his Spitfire over the English Channel.

Anyway, until the resting the joint had been jumping with in-house entertainment. The record player warmed us up, then Dad did a stint on the upright piano. Mum and Connie danced the Charleston. Their gold fringed flapper dresses shook and shimmied, courtesy of Mum's needlework skills of course.

Frankie Doyle entertained for an hour singing and twanging the strings on his guitar. He had a talent for twisting a song, making it different. Maybe a fast number slowed down, lingering over certain words, messing about with quavers and crotchets. Watching him, it was hard to believe he was generally kind of shy. I knew he was keen on me, toyed with the idea of getting matey with him. Problem was my heart didn't go pit-a-pat at the thought.

Old Ma Flowers supplied the comedy. She collared her Bert, the second husband, performed a lively version of the Sand Dance. He was lanky, thin as a wick, she as wide as she was high. It shouldn't have worked, but it did.

Vera performed her bog standard conjuring trick, magicked away an impressive amount of vodka. Nobody clapped or cheered. It was a worn routine we'd all seen too often.

Finally, Mr Doyle tuned up his penny whistle, took himself back to the Emerald Isles. I perched on the arm of Mum's chair. She nursed a cherry brandy, watched Uncle Stavros. He begged Liverpool Lou to behave like other girls do. It made a change from his usual Sinatra renditions.

The fire spluttered a protest behind its metal guard. Coals shifted. I shifted my peepers around the room, stabilised them on the settee arrangement. The three seater held five behinds. On the left, Maureen from the Co-op cuddled up to Billy the tattooed lorry driver. To the right Grace and Duffy played footsie, a Mona Lisa smile on her lips, him with a grin as if he'd won the Pools. Vera squashed in the middle, there at least in body. It was plain the mind was someplace else. I wondered where she'd gone to, wondered if there had ever been a love of her life.

Denny led the dolly bird past my line of vision. She smelled of Chantilly scent, he of soap and scotch. I understood the attraction, that heavy length of hair the shade of barley, those knee high boots a mile from a knife pleated skirt. She dangled a Babycham by its neck in her free hand, had carted it about all evening. I hoped she wouldn't be a pushover. Maybe then Denny would tire of her quicker. Or maybe he'd take it as a challenge. Either way she was on a hiding to nowhere.

I heard a rat-a-tat-tat on the front door, glanced at Dad, expected him to do the honours.

He was deep in a debate with Uncle Stavros. From where I was perched it appeared sizzling hot, finger jabbing from Dad, arm gesturing from Uncle. So I did the honours, prayed it wouldn't be Mr O'Connor from number fifteen complaining. He was a Jehovah, didn't believe in Christmas or much else. Dad said if he came Bible bashing tonight he'd give him a punch up the bracket. Mum said that wasn't very Christian.

I opened the door. Jesus filled the space. I think I'd better explain.

It happened a fortnight ago, early evening, cold enough to ice the windows. Kids retired inside without being summoned. Mum caught me before I could shrug of my coat, thrust a heap of season's greetings into my grubby mitt, suggested I post them pronto. She ignored the grumbles of complaint, gave me a glare not worth arguing with. I continued grumbling on my way out, took the threat of a clip round the lughole with me to the line of shops at the end of our road.

Shopkeepers were closing down for the day. Last minute losers were leaving the bookies. The aroma of fish and chips frying had my taste buds working overtime. I fancied a tanners worth of scraps, wished I'd had the sense to try a bit of bargaining for the inconvenience.

I posted the season's greetings, dipped hands into pockets; put a foot off the kerb. That's when the grey saloon clipped me. It spun me westwards, dumped me in the gutter. I lay front up, stunned, staring at an navy blue sky spoiled by chimney smoke. Seconds later a face blocked the view. I stared at that instead. It belonged to a man, dark hair long enough to caress the collar of a greatcoat. The eyes were black, skin the colour of Demerara sugar. A nine o'clock shadow covered the chin, the top lip. I'd seen that face before, in a stained glass window at the Baptist Church.

"Are you Jesus?" I said.

"No kid, I'm not Jesus," he said.

I propped myself on one elbow, took a gander about. In my hour of need nobody was on hand.

"You ran me over." I cautiously made it to upright, relieved to find no damage to limbs or torso.

"You didn't check the coast was clear." He straightened his spine, winced at the effort.

I noted he was pushing on in years, at least as many as my Dad. The creases in his skin were a giveaway.

I snuck a once over. He was tall, broad shouldered. The beginning of fear tickled the fine hairs at the nape of my neck. I stepped to the right. He stepped with me. I stepped to the left. He stepped too. We did the stepping game some more until I stopped. He smiled, showed a perfect set of pearly whites.

"Sure you're okay?" He stepped forward. A whiff of Old Spice accompanied him.

My ticker began to beat a little harder, a little faster. I swiftly considered my options. They were pretty limited. I chose the safest one, ran like billy-o back home, didn't stop till the kitchen door was shut tight. As an extra precaution I turned the key in the lock, shot the bolts top and bottom. From the lounge Mr. Laine suggested keeping the doggies rollin'. Rawhide was set to hit the dusty trail. I draped my coat over a kitchen chair, slipped my shoes beneath. As I joined my parents, Rowdy Yates cantered across the screen.

"You weren't long," Mum said.

"No, I ran," I said.

"Eager for that clip round the ear, Joan, that's what she is," Dad said.

That's when I decided not to mention the encounter with the grey saloon, decided it wasn't worth the lecture I was bound to get on the safety of road crossing. Of course I didn't know Jesus would be resurrected at our front door ten minutes to midnight on New Year's Eve, did I? But there he stood. And what's more, he wasn't in the least shocked to see me, was smiling that pearly white smile of his before it slid of his face. The replacement sent chills skittering north along my backbone. Even then I couldn't drag my peepers off his. But that's the problem with fear, isn't it. There's a 50-50 chance it'll root you to the spot.

"Fetch your dad," he said. "Tell him his old army buddy Jack is here."

It took mere seconds for my memory to dredge to the surface a particular earwigging incident, the one that sure as hell fire scared the living daylights out of me when I was nine.

Now that crazy son of a you know what had his toes nudging our threshold, the wind flapping his unbuttoned greatcoat like the wings of a giant bird. My heart beat so hard I thought it might break through the rib cage, leave me stone cold dead. For half a second I wondered if heaven really was that short of a sunbeam.

"What's wrong, kid?" The crazy son of a you know what bent at the waist, lowered himself to my level. A tic tugged at his left nostril. "You want some niceties first? Maybe we could shake hands, exchange a few words of small talk."

I peeled my tongue away from the roof of its mouth, did what any kid would do, put both feet in reverse.

"I'll get my dad," I said.

Fortunately, Dad was already on his way. We dosey doh-ed past one another in the hall. I tucked myself behind the ten foot shadow he made on the carpet, used the lounge door as a shield. My left lughole heard a velvet tone off the radio reporting from Trafalgar Square. The other one stayed tuned to the goings-on at front of house.

"This better be a social visit, Jack," Dad said.

I slid a peeper free of the shield.

"What other kind is there, Mickey?"

But he was lying through his pearly whites. There was nothing social about his visit that night, 'cos by the light of the moon I clearly saw the silver shape of a gun pulled from the innards of his greatcoat.

"God in heaven, Jack." Dad rocked on his heels. I rocked on mine.

"See this?" Jack held the gun skywards, forefinger probably trigger-happy for all I knew. After all, no sane person waved a shooter at the stars like some cowboy from one of those Westerns Dad was partial to, would they. At least not in my neck of the woods, I can assure you.

"Yeah, I see it," Dad said.

"It once played a game of Russian roulette. Remember that, Mickey?"

"I remember. What's this about, Jack? "

"It's about the game of chance, me old mucker."

Dad squared his shoulders, stretched out a hand, curled fingers beckoning. "Give me the gun, Jack, and stop talking in riddles."

"Best I keep it, if it's all the same to you. Who knows, it might come in handy."

I watched the gun arc north; disappear into the folds of Jack's coat. He withdrew a yard off the threshold.

"Handy for what, Jack?" Dad said.

"Get back to the club, Mickey, your baby brother's messing with the big boys."

He turned tail. I heard the crunch of footfalls on frost as he took his leave, heard the intake of air behind me, the smell of vodka vapours, knew the person breathing in my ear could only be Vera.

"Black Jack Baloo." Her voice was soft. I almost missed the reverence in it, as if Jesus Christ Almighty himself had graced us with a personal appearance. Black Jack faltered, then continued walking, fading into the darkness of a winter's night. As the door closed on a scene I wished I hadn't witnessed, the boom of foghorns in the harbour surfed inland.

"Come on, you two, you'll miss the toast." Mum thrust a wine glass at Vera, a tumbler of something watered down at me. We slipped further into the lounge. "Where's your father buggered off to now, eh? Bloody hell, he's never here when I need him."

"I'm always here when you need me, Joan." I stole a peep in Dad's direction. He was all smiles and swagger, as if he'd never just had an exchange of words with a gun toting crazy man. I peeped at Vera. She wore a fake smile fixed upon her Rimmel smudged lips.

"Happy New Year, Mickey Blackbee." Mum snaked an arm round his waist, kissed him on the mouth. He was happy to participate in the smackeroo.

We swept into a circle for the end of year ritual. I went through the words of Auld Lang Syne, hokey-cokeyed out the front door, in the back, but my heart wasn't in it, I was too busy worrying 'bout Uncle Stavros messing with the big boys, maybe playing Russian Roulette. More drinks were poured, more toasts were drank, more resolutions made only to be broken. I moved restlessly from merry maker to merry maker, received hugs, returned hugs, till I found myself on the outskirts beside Mr Doyle. He looked teary eyed. Guinness sometimes did that to him.

"Are you all right, Mr Doyle?" I said.

"I see black horses and pretty women weeping," he sighed.

"Crikey Mr Doyle, are you having a vision right this very minute?" I'd never been a spectator at a vision before, wondered if we should link hands, help make the connection to the spirit world stronger. I wondered if it was similar to the ones he had about the gee-gees running in the two-thirty at Doncaster. If so, it was bound to be the Guinness talking, 'cos Mr Doyle was cursed with matters concerning the race track.

"He won't make old bones," he said. "'Tis a rotten shame that."

"Who won't?" But even as I asked I knew who he meant, 'cos I followed the path his eyes had taken, all the way to Uncle Stavros.

4

I **stood beside Mr** Doyle with my beady eyeballs firmly fixed on Uncle Stavros in case he dropped dead. It didn't seem odds-on, 'cos though the party was winding down, he was still chock-a-block with the old charm, still putting on the razzmatazz, still spinning a nice line of saucy banter. Despite being on the short side, and not particularly gifted with the good looks, he was a renowned womaniser. Even the most hardened of straight-laced ladies found a rogue giggle gurgling in their throats. Even Vera came over all flirtatious when he moseyed into town. In fact, I got sick of hearing her chat him up as if she stood a chance.

Only Mum was immune to his powers of attraction. Most times it was obvious she couldn't stand the sight of him. Sometimes her gaze would linger his way longer than needed. Like it was doing then, at half past midnight, when worse for wear revellers were taking an age to leave. I thought I glimpsed a shadow of regret pass across her face. The thought unsettled me. Didn't I have enough to fret over with Mr Doyle's vision fresh on my mind?

Uncle concentrated his powers on Maureen from the Co-op, invited her to join him in a bit of rock-n-roll. She declined the invitation, which was just as well, she wasn't dressed for the occasion, not wearing that bum skimming black and white number Mum had knocked up on the Singer. Her boyfriend Billy wasted energy warning off the invitee with a menacing glare. He should have saved himself the effort; she was destined for somebody else anyways, somebody I trusted was mine.

Connie collected Mr Doyle from my side, led him home by the hand the way mothers do their kids. I hadn't seen the going of Grace and Duffy, nor Denny and the dolly bird, nor did I care. I was past caring, had the weight of the vision on my shoulders. It was too heavy a burden for a fifteen year old to carry alone. I wished I'd never witnessed it.

Dad cupped Granny Bee's elbow, planned to escort her to the spare bedroom. With courage supplied via a bottle of Harveys Bristol Cream she had other plans, had fraternised all evening with Mr Shaw whose memory remained in 1943, so now she was keen to sign up for the French Resistance. Too much sherry and war talk played havoc with her reasoning.

Vera flitted here and there clearing the festive fallout, the left-over nibbles, the abandoned paper party hats. Tom Jones accompanied her with a song about the green green grass of home. The story suited my blue blue mood.

I wandered into the kitchen, filled a cup with tap water, drank it neat. Through the twin hatch doors I caught sight of Uncle Stavros slopping a hefty measure of whiskey over ice.

The smog of fag smoke began to lift, hovered close to the ceiling like a storm cloud. Behind the fire guard the coals had burnt themselves out, along with the remainder of Christmas cheer. Mum returned from waving off the last of the stragglers, chanced upon Uncle downing a sneaky tot.

"Haven't you had enough of the devil's brew, Stavros?" Her tone sounded less than friendly.

"Don't get mad at me, Joanie." He sipped, eyed her over the rim of the glass. "Not tonight, eh."

"I'm not mad at you." She laughed a brittle laugh. "Why should I be?"

"You know why, you know how it is with me." He knocked back the rest of the whiskey, poured another.

Well, I didn't know why, didn't know how it was for him, but I did have the inclination to put two and two together, came up with one uncomfortable calculation. Was it possible, maybe even from the beginning, both the Blackbee brothers were in love with my mother?

My heart started banging louder than bongo drums in Borneo. It was a revelation. I couldn't believe I hadn't twigged the obvious, hadn't seen the hand resting too often on Mum's, the lingering hugs, Uncle tenderly tucking an unruly curl of hair behind her ear, 'cos of course I had seen all that, many times. I could list more, though I'm sure you get the gist of it, don't you? Problem was, did that prove she was the cheating kind?

Uncle Stavros' voice captured my attention from its unwelcome meandering.

"Joanie," he said, "I'm a naughty boy."

Peeping through the hatch, I watched him walk the swagger of a gunslinger towards Mum. She watched him too, stood taller. He traced a finger down her bare arm.

"Yes," she said, "you always are."

"What shall we do about it then, Joanie, hmmm?"

I heard a breath catch. It wasn't mine. A sharp elbow knocked me east. Vera replaced me at the hatch. It was safe to assume she was as angry as a housebound hornet.

"You'll bloody well do nothing about it," she said. "Party's over, Stavros, get yourself gone before I gives you the pasting of your life. And don't think I won't, 'cos I will, so help me God, and I'm in a right temper for it, an' all."

She slammed the twin doors shut, turned to me. It was not a friendly face she wore. I pedalled backwards till the Welsh dresser stopped me, briefly wondered if Uncle Stavros met his maker from a pasting from Vera.

"And you." She jabbed a forefinger in my direction. I noticed the nail was broken, the varnish chipped. "You should be in bed, you sneaky little earwigging toerag, instead of hiding in here up to no good."

I made a split decision to stand my ground against such unfair accusations. After all, I hadn't done anything, had only needed a drink. It was hardly my fault Uncle Stavros was still under the influence of the devils brew, was still working on his womanising ways.

"I haven't done anything," I said. "I only needed a drink of water."

Immediately, I pretty much knew it was the wrong decision. Vera took on the look of someone ready to blow a gasket. I took on the look of a coward, made a hasty exit. She followed hot on my heels. We met Mum in the hall. She engaged us in an eyeball wrestle.

Wisely, I let my peepers drop, concentrated on my slippers. Vera wasn't as smart. Whilst they sized each other up I made a break for freedom, scaled the stairs two at a time until I reached the third step from the top. If I squatted I could view them between the banisters. So I did.

"Well," Vera said, "let's get the rest of this mess cleared."

"Leave it till tomorrow," Mum said.

"It is tomorrow, Joan."

"Then leave it till later, Vera, I want my bed."

"Go then, I'm not stopping you, am I?"

I smirked as Mum adopted the position for battle. Her hands clutched at her waist, elbows akimbo. She planted her stocking feet apart, puffed out her chest. A tongue lashing was about to hit Vera smack bang in the chops.

"What the bloody hell's the matter with you, Vera Williams? Come on, let's have it. Then I'm going to kick your backside out that front door with my size fives."

"All right." Vera adopted the same battle stand. "I'll tell you what the bloody hell's the matter with me, Joan Blackbee. We should have taken that dead crow seriously, that's what we should have done. Now look what's happened."

"Nothing's happened. I wouldn't touch him with a pair of Marigolds." Mum snapped out every word with as much contempt as she could muster.

"I don't mean that skirt chaser Stavros, Joan, though God knows I saw what I saw and you know it. I mean Jack. He was here, talking to Mickey, and he promised, he did, not to ever show up, and he wouldn't break a promise, not after that awful, awful day." Vera sandwiched her face between her palms, took in a gulp of air.

"Jack? What did he want? Oh Christ, Vera, what a shock. Are you okay?" I heard the sound of soft crying. Mum closed the space between them, wrapped Vera in a two armed hug. The battle was over before it had begun.

"That crow's an omen, Joan, it's brought us bad history, the worse bloody sort an' all."

"Mickey will smooth it over, Vera. Don't worry."

"No, he mustn't go there, Joan. This isn't the usual Stavros shenanigans, not for Jack to break a promise." The on-set of panic wobbled her vocal chords.

"Stop it, Vera." Mum had her by the shoulders, gave her a shake. "Mickey will sort it.

Anyway, who says Stavros is involved this time? I'll tell you something though, I'll be glad when we're rid of that club. It's a bloody albatross."

I listened to Vera snuffling, Mum hushing. My mind was galloping faster than the winner of The Grand National. What happened to Vera on that awful, awful day? How was Black Jack involved? Why should Dad want rid of the club that wasn't his? And when would Uncle Stavros pack in his shenanigans?

"There's another thing you need to know, Joan."

"Don't you dare mention that ruddy crow again, Vera."

"No, I won't. This is worse."

"How could it be any worse than it already is?"

"Your daughter knows something of everything that went on tonight. That's how worse it is."

"Ye Gods preserve us. You mean the Jack thing?"

"Yes, but I'm not sure how long she was earwigging on that for."

"And the Stavros thing?"

"I'm certain she knows all about that little exchange. What are you going to say if she asks questions?"

"Tell her to mind her own bees' wax, that's what. Holy Mary, it's a complete and utter shambles, isn't it?"

"There's one other thing, Joan."

"Let me guess, Vera. Is it you're too scared to be on your tod tonight?"

"I'm too scared to be on my tod tonight. Can I stay here?"

Mum made a show of careful consideration. Vera swiped a sleeve across her face, rubbed knuckles in her eye sockets.

"I suppose, but you'll have to top and tail with Ruby. The place is like a refuge for dropouts already."

"The past won't ever let us go, will it, Joan?" She caught a hold of Mum's hand.

"No, it won't. We'll just have to live with it. We've survived so far, haven't we?"

Together they turned to climb the stairs. I scooted to my pit, tumbled beneath the sheets fully clothed, faced the wall. The bedroom door opened. I screwed my eyelids down tight, evened out my breathing, relaxed my limbs.

"I think she's a-kip," Mum whispered. "Now, try to sleep, perhaps things will be clearer in the morning."

I felt the bedclothes lift. Vera slipped in the bottom of my single divan. A draught of cold air slipped in with her.

"I very much doubt it, Joan. That dead crow wasn't on your garden path for nothing."

"I thought I told you not to mention the ruddy crow again."

"But it's bothering me, isn't it, been bothering me all day."

"And I'll bother you some more if you don't shut up and go to sleep."

Within minutes the sound of snoring came yodelling through Vera's nostrils. I unscrewed my eyelids. The curtains weren't drawn; the door was left ajar, the landing light burning electricity 'cos the dark and I weren't compatible. A slice of pale orange cut across the rose coloured carpet. Outside a milky moon sat perfectly still in the night sky.

Carefully, I snuck out of bed, crept to the window, peered through the glass. To the left I glimpsed Denny disappear through the Doyle's back door, wondered why it took so long to walk the dolly bird home, what favours he expected, what favours she'd given.

To the right Mr Steven Shaw marched the length of the garden, about turned, marched again. I recalled the stories he told me of Sonny Jim. His proper name was Stanley James, a farmer's boy, who never made it home. If I close my peepers I can picture him, the yellow hair, the ready smile, the hands the size of shovels, the capers they got up to before they were captured. But it wasn't really a story, it was all true, and Sonny Jim was Steven's friend.

Mr Shaw's brother Philip came to guide him inside, reassured him the war was over. He'd been a conscientious objector, done a stretch in prison for his beliefs, mainly kept himself to himself. Mum said a lot of people were broken before the fighting stopped, and not all of them were on the front line.

With nothing else to reflect upon, I rewound the evening's events. To be honest, I didn't need to wait for morning for things to be clearer. As far as I was concerned it couldn't be any more crystal. For starters, Vera and Jack with the gun were partners in a tragedy. Dad had greater clout in the Soho club than I'd been led to believe. Signs were Mum walked a rocky road between two brothers. Uncle Stavros was neck high in deep shit. And if that weren't plenty to be going on with, I felt sure more secrets were ready for confession, were dangerously teetering on the lips of my nearest and dearest. Probably more than Father Francis from the Catholic Church ever had the privy to hear. And now I was a keeper of secrets too, 'cos nobody knew I'd witnessed Mr Doyle's vision, or seen that gun.

The mantelpiece clock in the lounge chimed twice. I returned to bed, snuck extra carefully back in. The cold of winter had seeped through to the marrow. I'd have welcomed a hot water bottle like a long lost bosom buddy.

"I knew you weren't asleep." Vera propped herself on one elbow. "What's the matter? The light's on and I'm here, so there's nothing to be afraid off."

"I'm not afraid," I said.

"Get some shut-eye then. No doubt your father will be bugling reveille at some stupid hour of the morning."

"I would get some shut-eye, Vera, if you stopped talking."

"Don't try and be clever with me, young lady, or I'll give you one of me famous Chinese burns."

I'd once been on the receiving end of a famous Chinese burn, didn't fancy a repeat experience, decided on a change of tactics. Perhaps, since she was drenched in vodka, she'd be willing to part with a little information.

"Do you want to share my pillows?" I said.

"What's in it for you?" she said.

"Answers," I said.

"I've got no answers, Ruby, none that'll make any sense. Now, give me a pillow."

"No."

She stole one anyway, plumped it up, settled her bottle blonde hair upon it. I pulled down my blinkers, hoped sleep would quickly take me into the land of nod. It did, along with the certainty that the balance of fate was most definitely tipping the wrong way.

5

No bugling reveille at some stupid hour woke me the next day. The morning light through open curtains did the job instead. I sent out a toe to explore the bottom of the single divan.

It reported back the absence of another body. To double check I sent my peepers north, saw a dent in the pillow where Vera had been. That meant one thing only. The grown-ups had already parley-voused about the fiasco of last night. With my spirits licking the soles of my slippers I made my way downstairs, avoided the creaky second step, picked up the words of a three-sided conversation coming from the kitchen.

"So what's the plan?" Vera said.

"There isn't a plan," Mum said.

"Then you better think of one quick, Joan, before he finds himself wrestling on the ropes."

"I've got a plan," Dad said. "Let him sort his own problems out, he's bloody old enough."

"Mickey." Mum's voice sounded wheedling. "He's your brother. You must do something. And there's the matter of mother to consider. She's fragile, Mickey, how will she cope if, well, just if?"

"Oh for God's sake, Joan, why did you have to mention mother, eh? Suppose I'll have to go the weekend now. I'm telling you though, he's getting a kick right up the jacksy when I catch him, bloody sneaking off before I could give him what's what."

"And there's Jack too," Vera said.

"Yes, Mickey," Mum said. "There's Jack too."

I inched closer to the kitchen, forgot the squeaky floorboard in the hall. It delivered forth the warning of enemy approaching, alerted the plotters of my presence, informed them I'd deliberately skipped the creaky second step. My foot dithered mid-air for a second before it continued onwards.

"Big Ears is on her way," Dad said. "She forgot the squeaky floorboard, must be losing her touch."

"Remember what we agreed, don't let her try any of her tricks," Mum hissed.

I made an appearance at the door, greeted their smiles with a teeth bared snarl, took myself over to the eyelevel grill. Toast was on the menu for breakfast.

"And aren't we fortunate she's in such a sweet mood, Joan?" Dad soaked every syllable with sarcasm. I concentrated on the bread browning, preferred it barely golden with oodles of butter. I noticed the twin-tub filled with water, ready for action.

"I'll be off then," Vera said.

"And I've got beds to strip," Mum said.

I sat at the table, bit into breakfast, primed my peepers on Dad. He busied himself with an old Daily Mail, re-read stale news. A full cup of coffee stood abandoned in its saucer. I helped myself, shuddered as it rolled over the tongue. If I'd known it was Vera's I wouldn't have troubled. She drank coffee thick as tar, sweet as syrup. It clung to my molars, coated my tonsils like mildew on damp. I tasted a tang of something other than Maxwell House, something suspicious. I tried another sip to verify my suspicions. I was right. She was already topping herself up with whiskey. As vodka was her usual tipple the outcome of that indulgence seemed bleak. She would probably go off the rails, would need drying out, would expect Mum to help her with the DT's.

I renewed the beady eyeballing. Dad finally folded the paper, laid it on the table, smoothed it flat. He sighed, rubbed calloused hands through his hair, looked me straight in the eye. I looked straight back without blinking.

"What do you want to know, Ruby?" he said.

"Promise to tell the truth, Dad," I said.

"I always tell the truth, me darlin'."

My belly danced a frisky fandango. I wavered for a while, arranged my questions in an orderly queue, decided on a slow build to the one I most wanted an answer to. Why was Black Jack Baloo at our front door with a shooter?

"I'm waiting, Ruby." Dad rolled a fag with the fingers of one hand, tucked it between his lips, flicked the little wheel on the Zippo. The smell of lighter fluid blended perfectly with Sun Valley baccy. He raised eyebrows at me like he does when his patience is wearing thin. I narrowed my peepers, changed tactics, went for the element of surprise.

"Why was Black Jack Baloo at our front door with a shooter?" I said.

His eyebrows dipped, pulled together, formed a frown. He cocked his head west, blew smoke out the east side of his mouth, had another drag.

"Well, well, well." He leaned back against the chair, whistled low through his teeth.

"You said you always tell the truth, Dad." My heart stepped it up a pace. The old wall clock ticked away the time. If he didn't answer soon Mum would return with an armful of washing for the twin-tub.

"So I did," he said.

"What is the truth then?" I said.

"The truth is, Ruby me darlin'," he tilted forward, glued cold grey eyes on mine, "I'll bloody skin you alive if you ever mention that again, understood?"

It was my turn to lean back, to put space between us. Neither one of us broke the eye lock. I heard Mum singing in the hall, a song from a musical she had a soft spot for, about a secret love she once had. I wondered if she thought of Uncle Stavros while she sang.

"Understood, Ruby?" Dad reached out, covered my fist with a calloused palm.

"Yes." I pulled away. He tightened his grip.

"Good." His fingers loosened. Hands slipped apart. Eyes did not.

Mum bustled through the door, white cotton sheets sweeping across the tiles. We swivelled our heads towards her. She dumped the pile on the floor, lifted the twin-tub's lid, shook in a helping of Daz. Perfume wafted on the air as the powder hit hot water.

"I don't know why I'm bothering," she said. "Who's to know these sheets have only been slept on once."

"You're too fussy, Joan," Dad vacated his seat, placed his cup on the drainer.

"Maybe I am, Mickey, but I won't have anyone tittle-tattling about the state of my bedding." She gathered the wash, had a sniff. "Anyway, I can still smell Granny Bee's Soir de Paris on this pillowslip."

My peepers rolled a circuit in their sockets. I also placed my plate and Vera's unfinished coffee on the drainer, almost escaped.

"Before you disappear, Ruby, take this plate next door." Mum dunked the bundle into the suds. Fragrant steam circled round her. "Connie forgot it, what with that man of hers as plastered as he was."

I toyed with the idea of refusing. Returning the plate would mean running into Mr Doyle. What if he recalled the vision, the black horses, pretty women weeping. What if he recalled the path his eyes had taken, all the way to Uncle Stavros. What if he remembered it was me there beside him.

"Oh for goodness sake, child, stop your daydreaming," Mum said. "When I was your age I didn't have a spare minute for dreaming, I was working. Bloody kids nowadays don't know when they're well off, do they, Mickey?"

"No, they don't, Joan, shower of twerps, the lot of 'em."

My peepers rolled again. When they stopped I found them focused on Mum. She threw me a black look. I lobbed one of my own. They clashed and held. I read a tip in hers. It advised me to back-pedal fast. I picked up the Doyle's plate with the fluted rim, took the easy way out. In the hall my feet stalled, my lugholes readied themselves for an earwigging.

I heard nothing but water sloshing in the twin-tub, sucked in a breath, prepared myself for the meeting with Mr Doyle, left the front door on the latch.

In the street the wail of a motorbike getting its guts revved greeted me. As usual, my belly performed a triple flip at the sight of Denny astride the clapped out Tiger Cub. I gave him the once over. He was as lovely as ever, especially his hair brushing the collar of a leather jacket. Nobody else had hair like his. It practically begged me to reach for a handful, to let my fingers comb through the tangled curls. My lungs heaved a sigh. I watched a slow smile grace the corners of his mouth. A sneer tugged at mine. I hugged the plate to my chest, started down the path.

"Alright, Ruby?" he said.

"Never better," I said.

"Wanna take a ride; feel the wind in that red hair of yours?" He patted the petrol tank.

"On that death trap of yours? You got to be joking." I hoisted the plate higher, along with my chin. "I've more important things to do."

"What more important things? It's Boxing Day, there's nothing to do."

"Then go and do nothing with your girlfriend, Denny, I'm sure she'll be delighted to see you, 'cos I sure as hell aren't."

"It didn't work out with her." The engine stuttered, fell silent. A strong smell of burning oil drifted away on the cold breeze. He cocked his leg over the seat, leaned the bike on its stand.

"Seemed to be working out just fine last night." Behind my ribs the heart tapped out a little dance.

"Nah, she's not my type after all."

"So what's your type then?" I kept my voice edged with boredom.

"Maybe someone like you." He upped the smile to full voltage. His lips parted company. I noticed a slight overbite, raised my peepers to his baby blues, missed the warning of danger clearly visible in them, mistook it for desire.

"Really?" I hated the sound of hope I wrapped around the word, immediately knew I'd set myself up for a tumble. My teeth clamped together tight. I rolled my hands into fists.

"Only maybe, Ruby." He laughed. It was loaded with scorn. I scraped together as much dignity as I possibly could.

"Yeah, and only maybe I'd be interested." I gave a snort followed by a shoulder twitch, wondered if he could see my heart bleeding beneath my cardie, wondered if he would even care. I glanced down; half expected to see a crimson stain there.

Denny tipped forward, still smiling. Our peepers had barely an inch width of fresh air between them.

"You'd be interested," he said.

His breath was hot on my face. It smelled of Wrigley's gum. I had the urge to drop the nut on that perfect straight nose of his. Before I could put the urge into action, he dodged west, held the gate open for me to pass through. I stayed rooted, had the inclination for a little revenge if violence was off the agenda.

"Take your Mum's plate." I thrust the plate with the fluted rim at him. He reached for it. My fingers let go before his got a hold. It smashed to smithereens on the pavement. I watched his baby blues widen. He wasn't smiling any more.

"Jesus, Ruby, that's one of her best plates," he said.

"Next time you take me for a fool, Denny Doyle, I'll break a four-be-two over your head."

I began the walk home. Anger helped me along, which was just as well, 'cos tears were balancing on the edge of my lower eyelids. The winter chill seeped through my cardie. I hugged arms across my chest.

"Hey, Ruby," Denny said.

I spared him a glance. A wry smile played across his face.

"You're something else, girl, you know that?"

"Yeah, so are you, Doyle. You're something horrible," I said.

His laugh chased me indoors. I wasted a moment, composed myself, heard the twin-tub tumbling the sheets around in the drum, heard the whistler building up to a boil, heard Dad say, "Don't upset yourself, Joan, not over Stavros. He's got the luck of the devil, he has."

But Dad's confidence was short-lived. Uncle Stavros' luck ran out.

6

There was a heated debate concerning my attendance at Uncle Stavros' funeral. On one side stood Mum. She put her case forward, leaned heavily towards protection of a minor. On the other side Dad supported the traditional paying of last respects. It appeared I had little say in the matter. The debate lobbied back and forth for days, even as we waited for Vera to turn up for the departure to Soho.

"She's not coming, Mickey Blackbee." Mum slapped her hands upon the table. Chin jutting, she tipped forward, glared at Dad. "She can stay at the Doyle's. And that is final."

"For Christ's sake, Joan," Dad said. "It's only right she pays her last respects. She's not a child anymore."

"And what good will it do, eh? She's been hurt enough. And what if she hears things? Haven't thought about that, have you? It's not just the funeral I'm talking about here, and you know it."

"I know what you're talking about, Joan, and she's old enough to decide for herself. Probably do her a favour an' all, stop her viewing life through those rose-tinted glasses she's taken to wearing lately."

At that point Vera tottered in. We checked her out. It was obvious she'd indulged in a hefty drop of something strong to help her through the day. Without a word of greeting they picked up where they'd left off.

"But it's the club, Mickey. We agreed to keep what happened before to ourselves."

"Then perhaps we were wrong. I'm not ashamed of what happened before, Joan, I'm not ashamed of anything."

Well, that ruffled my interest, I can tell you. I noticed Mum gather her many indignities together, noticed her nostrils flare, her lips tighten. Sometimes she took umbrage at the least little thing. Sometimes it worked to my advantage. Sometimes pieces of secrets slipped out between angry words. Unfortunately, she took it personally, went on the attack.

"Then you're a fool, Michael George Blackbee, a bloody fool who's learned nothing."

Mum's voice was dangerously controlled. Her eyebrows arched, practically reached the hairline. I cast my peepers to the back of beyond. Once they'd returned and settled, I rolled my head west. Dad stalled for time, opened his tin of Sun Valley baccy. A muscle twitched in his jaw, a clear indication he was fighting a losing battle with patience.

"I've learned a lot, Joan." He kept his sight on Mum, lit up the gasper, blew out a column of smoke. "I learned to live with my sins, to survive. My brother didn't. He's dead."

I heard Mum draw in a deep breath, felt the build up of tears on my lower eye-lids, blinked them over the edge. She wrapped me in a bear hug. The scent of cheap market perfume leaked through her black twin-set. Her string of freshwater pearls pressed cool against my brow. I wrenched my face free, saw Dad's twisted with grief, saw Vera place a hand on his forearm, give it a pat. I couldn't bear it, couldn't bear the whole sorry mess we were in any longer. My Uncle's tragedy had taken more than just himself away, hadn't it? It had taken my Dad away too. And I missed him. I missed his easy laugh, his answer for everything tripping off his tongue, his whistling along to the radio. If I'd had the guts I would have hated my one and only Uncle for dying.

"Oh God, Mickey," Mum whispered. "What are we going to do?"

I squirmed in Mum's arms, gave a tearful hiccup. She wiped a tear away with the pad of her thumb.

"We're going to bury my brother, Joan, that's what we're going to do."

"But Mickey, can't you see the bloody awful state she's in already? It'll be worse at the graveside, won't it, when all that's left is a pile of dirt and a few useless prayers."

"Let her decide, Joan. I'm tired of arguing about it."

I sensed Dad's resolve wavering. Panic stirred in my belly. If I didn't stick my oar in soon I'd be dumped on the Doyle's, would never have the chance to hear the things Mum definitely didn't want me hearing. And not only that, I agreed with Dad, it was only fitting I paid my last respects to Uncle Stavros, the man who used to dance the soft shoe shuffle, the singer of Sinatra songs. I squeezed out a few crocodile tears for extra effect, had learned long ago those little beauties could sway a parent's heart.

"I want to go, Mum; I want to pay my last respects." I wailed like a cat squaring up for a fight.

"So she's coming then, is she?" Vera said.

"Yes, she is" Dad said. "We bury my brother as a family should, and that's my final word on the matter."

"Well, that's that then." Mum straightened her spine, clattered cups and saucers together, sniffed her disapproval. "Mickey's made a decision, though why he wants to start making them now is beyond me."

"It's Ruby's decision, Joan," Dad said. "Get ready; I'm hitting the road in five minutes."

"Best fetch the bags, hadn't I?" She gave Vera a nudge. "You can help, make yourself useful for a change."

I waited till their feet hit the creaky second step. Since it was a sure bet I had the go ahead to attend, something bothered me. I began fiddling with the hem of my school skirt. I'm a terrible fiddler when the worries get a hold of me. It was a childhood habit I hadn't managed to break. Dad reached across, stilled my fingers with his.

"What's bothering you now, Ruby?" he said.

"How upsetting will it be at the graveside?" I said.

"It'll be very upsetting." His fingers stayed on mine.

"Will you be crying, Dad?"

"No, I won't be crying."

"Is it okay if I do?"

"Of course it is. You cry all you want, me darlin', you won't be the only one. Why, it's practically expected at funerals." He gave me a reassuring smile. I noticed it was just a token gesture, didn't crinkle his eyes like the real McCoy. "But I won't be 'cos men don't cry. Didn't you know that?"

"Men are stupid then, aren't they, Dad?"

"We are, Ruby, very stupid indeed. By the way, those last few tears you dribbled were as fake as tattooed Billy's Rolex, weren't they?"

Thankfully Mum returned, saved me from trying out another white lie. She heaved in a bulging suitcase. Vera carried a box in her arms, a grimace on her face.

"What the bloody hell is Doyle doing dressed up like a penguin on the back of Denny's motorbike?" she said.

"What the bloody hell have you got in that suitcase?" Dad said. "For Christ's sake, Joan, we're only staying a night."

"Necessities, Mickey, that's what's in the suitcase. So what's Doyle doing, eh? I swear he's heading fast for the funny farm if Connie don't rein him in some."

We buttoned coats, trooped outside, waited while Dad deadlocked the front door. He marched off, suitcase swinging in his left hand. Mum shouldered the wood twice before she was satisfied it wouldn't cave in under pressure. Vera and I stalled on the step, knew what was coming next. We shoved hands into pockets, stamped our feet to keep the circulation from freezing up.

"Hold your horses, Mickey," Mum said. "Did you turn the gas off?"

"Yes, Joan." I heard the strain in Dad's reply. He put in another couple of strides, reached the gate.

"What about the back door?"

"Locked and bolted."

"Windows, Mickey, did you remember them?"

He retraced his footsteps, gave Mum a warning glare she chose to ignore. "Shut tight, Joan, let's go."

"Do you think the water needs turning off at the stopcock? It's brass monkey weather; don't want to come home to burst pipes, do we?"

I sighed. Vera sighed. Dad dropped the suitcase, rearranged the flat cap on his head.

"Holy Moses, Mother of God. Why do we have this bloody palaver every time we leave the bloody house? Why can't we be like normal people, Joan? It's a flipping rigmarole, that's what it is."

"There's no call to shout, Mickey." Mum shouldered the door once again. "You really mustn't scrimp on safety, must you. Anyway, what are you dithering around for? Let's find out what that mad fool Doyle is playing at."

The four of us single-filed along the garden path, lined up beside the pale blue Ford Cortina estate Dad had upgraded to. We fixed our peepers on the Doyle's. As usual Denny looked divine in a scuffed and studded leather jacket. His jeans were Levi's, fitted perfectly, no doubt lifted off a clothesline from not round here.

Mr Doyle's black suit was shiny with wear, his shirt an eye blinding white. He'd have easily passed for one of those smarmy door-to-door insurance reps flogging policies offering piss-poor returns, unless you took his hair into consideration. It gave the game away, being a very close likeness to a dandelion gone to seed. No smarmy self-appreciating rep would dare cold-call without the heavily oiled standard short back and sides.

"Where you going, Doyle, all dressed up like a penguin?" Dad said. "Denny got another court appearance?"

"That he has not," Mr Doyle said. "Me and the boy are representing my family on the sad loss of our friend Stavros. We'll tag on the end of the mourners, Mickey, we won't be intruding none."

I glanced at Dad, could tell he was touched with emotion 'cos his face wobbled a bit.

"I appreciate the gesture, Doyle," he said.

They shared a look that stayed frozen for seconds longer than it should have. Denny kick-starting the bike snapped their eyes apart. Dad cleared his throat, jiggled the car keys.

Mr Doyle made a cross the length and breadth of his pigeon chest, mumbled a prayer to some saint I failed to catch the name of. It was the prompt we needed to take our places in the Ford Cortina estate. I draped myself on the right hand side of the back seat, Vera parked her skinny behind on the left. Dad and Mum sat up front.

"Well," Dad said, "seems we got ourselves a pair of outriders escorting us to Soho."

Nobody found the urge to comment. I snuck a discreet peep at Denny, admired the width of his shoulders, the clever hands that whipped packets of Woodbines from Murphy's Corner Store. I was still pretty much smitten with him, still hoped he might one day turn his attention my way. Sometimes it was almost painful just to see him. Sometimes he treated me to a smile. Then his blue eyes bordering on mauve crumpled at the corners, dimples flashed in his cheeks. It was a fatal combination, had the potential to rob ripe and ready girls of their virginal virtues. Girls like me. Although, as things stood, it seemed highly unlikely. But I continued to hold on to hope 'cos I'm no quitter. That's the trouble with me. Even when I'm down and out I don't know when to throw the towel in.

I kept my peepers firmly fixed on the Triumph motorbike's flashing brake lights all the way to Soho. Then I kept them fixed on the club, a God awful pile of bricks as tacky as a two bob souvenir from Brighton seafront.

"Is this it?" I heard utter disbelief in the question. "Is this the club?"

"What did you expect then, Ruby," Dad said, "the sodding Ritz?"

He got out the car. I did too, took a good long look-see around. The narrow street was cobbled, both sides jam-packed with pubs and clubs and cafes. Neon signs snoozed the day away. The aroma of something spicy hit a bull's eye on my hooter. A crowd had gathered in front of Stan's Greasy Spoon. They stared in our direction. From within more faces peered through the plate glass window. I gave them my very best scowl. A postcard one door down read French lessons here.

"French lessons?" I said. "Who the flipping heck wants to learn French in a dump like this?"

"It's not that sort of French," Dad said.

Mum and Vera joined us on the pavement. A tall woman in tight black broke from the crowd, hip swayed forwards. She wore four inch heels, auburn hair backcombed high. A thick diamond choker circled her neck. A thin crimson mouth worked over a wad of chewing gum. I gave her a withering once over. She gave me a snarl, Vera a nod, Mum a hug, a kiss, another hug. My jaw dropped south when she spoke. The voice belonged to a forty fags a day Scouse docker.

"So, Mickey, this be the sprog then?" she said. "See she's inherited your attitude."

"Yep, chip of the old block, Big Shirley. Now, where's the Duchess?"

"She's inside. Sullivan's keeping an eye on her."

"How bad is the old girl, Shirley?" Mum said.

"Well, the quack's doped her up to the eyeballs. She don't know what day of the week it is, poor soul."

"Get the suitcase out the boot, Shirley." Dad fumbled with a set of keys, found the one he wanted. "We need to be ready. I'll bring the Duchess down."

I followed Dad into a sizeable square hall. The floor was black and white checked tiles.

A heavy duty door lay on the right. To the left, a staircase climbed the wall. Ahead, beneath a window, stood a highly polished sideboard lavished with mother-of-pearl. It looked foreign, maybe from some far flung land like India.

"Stay here," Dad said.

He took the stairs two at a time. I took a nosey out the window. Just a brick enclosed yard was on view. My peepers dropped to the collection of framed photographs displayed on the sideboard. Yours truly was missing. There was Mum and Dad, Uncle Stavros on his ownsome, a handsome, dusky skinned stranger I didn't know from Adam. I picked up a brown spotted picture in a brass frame. It was a wedding snap. The happy couple looked as miserable as sin. After a minute I recognised Granny Bee. She had been pretty in her heyday, heart shaped face, wide spaced eyes. I held it closer, studied the groom, my grandfather, for the first time. I noticed a strong likeness between him and Dad, the mouth, the chin, the stare that could freeze you in your tracks from twenty paces. I wondered why I'd never seen a photo before, or earwigged on any gossip. I wondered why I hadn't even thought to ask about him. But most of all, I wondered if he was another family secret.

I heard footfalls above, raised my peepers to the ceiling. I briefly appreciated the egg and dart coving. Then the strangest thing caught my full attention. A few feet away from the sideboard I noticed a hidden door, covered with the same fleur-de-lys paper as the walls.

I moved towards it, tried the tiny handle. It was unlocked, opened without a groan of protest.

I knew I shouldn't, but I inched it wider. That's when a long fingered hand covered mine, slammed it shut. I gave a faint cry of surprise, my heart quickened, my belly rolled the rumba.

"Nothing worth seeing in there," Big Shirley said in my lughole.

I pulled free, put some distance between us, heard the ring of horseshoes striking stone, hurried to see outside. Big Shirley followed. Along the street came two black horses, sleek as patent leather. From both sides of the street mourners fell in behind the carriage carrying Uncle Stavros on his final journey. A woman began to softly wail. Others followed suit. Men kept their emotions in check, removed hats, lit fags. Mr Doyle's vision was happening.

"Holy shit," Big Shirley said. I felt a hand rest upon my right shoulder. "I was still hoping it wasn't true."

7

The chapel was packed to the rafters. For many it was standing room only. I sat on the hard front row pew sandwiched between Dad and Big Shirley. Mum and Vera flanked Granny Bee. She looked a little bewildered. I wondered how she'd manage by herself at The Bee Hive. I wondered if she was silently screaming inside like me, if she too felt frozen through to the marrow. I wondered if the organist ever had a yearning to jazz up the solemn music.

The vicar took his place. Everyone hushed. All eyes settled on the small round man with the boozers nose, made red by broken capillaries. He began the show to send Uncle Stavros on his way to paradise, put plenty of hellfire into it as well. Hymns were sung with great enthusiasm. A firm amen echoed after prayers. Seemed to me my Uncle only had a slim chance of getting through those Pearly Gates. He'd broken at least three of the Ten Commandments that I knew of. I was glad when we set off on the pilgrimage to the chosen plot, in the shade of an ancient yew tree that had seen better days.

More than a hundred bodies muscled through Kensal Green All Souls. In pole position was the nearest and dearest. The six of us kept the same line-up as we had on that hard pew.

Behind came a bevy of mixed aged females, tottering on their high heels, sniffling into hankies. A cold breeze ruffled fur collared coats. Pieces of best jewellery flashed an SOS in the weak winter sun. Uncle Stavros had surely been a fine juggler of women to be loved by so many.

Pushing us on, couples and lone men added their weight to the cortege. My peepers searched for Black Jack. They couldn't find him. I wasn't surprised. After all, he was a wanted man, wasn't he? He was the man with the gun.

We marched en-masse like refugees, then circled the final resting place. A pile of dirt was heaped to one side ready for the backfill. More words were spoken. I mumbled my way through the Lord's Prayer. The funeral bearers carefully lowered the coffin. I watched it disappear. The vicar picked up a lump of earth, crumbled it into the grave. Ashes to ashes, dust to dust. Others followed suit. Some dropped flowers. I dropped Frank Sinatra in. He wasn't really mine to drop. He was my Christmas gift to Uncle Stavros. It seemed the right thing to do 'cos I didn't want anybody else to listen to that record ever again.

Mourners began to drift away. A couple of men with shovels hovered in the distance, waited for us to take our leave. But leaving was harder than we thought. Eventually Big Shirley said, "We better get going. I've done a buffet for the wake."

"We won't fit that lot in upstairs," Dad said.

"Then open the club, Mickey."

"The club's finished, Shirley. It can burn to the ground for all I care."

Mum and Big Shirley traded glances. I tried to interpret them. The code was beyond me.

"Now Mickey," Mum said. "Be reasonable. The club can be finished tomorrow. You can't let all your friends down. What kind of send off would that be?"

Dad struggled to be reasonable. I held my breath, hoped reason would win through. After all, it was the only chance I'd probably get of an inside butchers, wasn't it? The only chance to walk a while in my uncle's footsteps, to imagine him there, laughing that throaty laugh of his, the one that rumbled from the pit of his belly, the one as contagious as measles. I felt the tears welling again, blinked them into submission, stared up at a storm ready sky, prayed to God for a small favour. It wasn't much to ask for. Luckily, he was listening.

"I want a minute to myself when we get back then," Dad said.

"Of course," Mum said. "Take as long as you need."

"And when I'm ready, I'll open the front doors. It'll be for the last time."

"We'll be waiting Mickey," Big Shirley said. "Come on, Vera, let's lead the way. You got anything left in that secret stash of yours?"

"Not much," Vera said.

"Well hand it over, you old lush." Big Shirley waggled the fingers on her right hand.

Vera dug deep in a pocket, passed over the silver hip flask. We made the return journey in silence. I lost myself in memories I believed were long forgotten. I guess we all did. I guess we all rewound our special moments with Uncle Stavros before they faded once again.

At the club the crowd cluttered up the pavement, spilled over into the street. They parted like the Red Sea to let us through. Only Dad disappeared inside. I took on a spot of rubbernecking, lugholes pricked for snippets of info. But mouths were blab free. Denny was talking to an older man. I gave him the once over, estimated his age somewhere in the region of mid twenties. He carried a little beef, had a Beatles mop top. A thin silver scar zipped across a square chin. I sidled their way. He noticed. I stopped sidling. Our peepers met and held. His were a shade of muddy brown, saw everything there was to see. I saw nothing but danger.

"Who's she?" He tipped his head towards me.

My lips peeled over gums, formed a grimace. I rolled my peepers as high as possible. When they fell back into place, he was smiling. It was his only redeeming feature, 'cos as ugly goes this man had it pretty much covered. But the smile was wide, slightly crooked. His teeth were straight, the canines proud, like a wolf, or maybe a vampire.

"She's the Blackbee kid," Denny said.

His expression told me I was a nuisance. I was fast going off him. Before I could think of an obnoxious one liner, Frank Sinatra interrupted, told us the summer wind came blowing in. My eyelids drooped. In the darkness behind them I pictured Uncle Stavros. My heart suffered another cut. I wondered how much more it could stand before it decided enough was enough.

From somewhere in the crowd Big Shirley picked up the tune. Others joined in. The Bee Hive doors opened. The man with the muddy browns cupped my elbow, urged me forward. We went in singing. I kept my peepers wide open, didn't want to miss a single solitary thing. The first thing they noticed was the glitter ball slowly spinning, scattering soft pastel shapes over the dimly lit club. Upfront, two steps high, a small stage lay empty. A row of naked white lights marked its boundary. On ground level a parquet dance floor needed polishing. To the right a juke box glowed blue. Upholstered booths the colour of Bourneville skirted the perimeter. Round tables with padded chairs filled in the spare space. On the left a cherry wood bar stretched itself out. Polished bronze pumps stood at ease. Spirit bottles hung bottoms up, wine and brandy glasses dangled by their stems. Dad was stationed behind the bar. I gave him the beady eye. He looked as if he belonged there, had discarded his suit jacket, loosened off his tie. Shirt sleeves were rolled to the elbows, collar unsnapped. He splashed Southern Comfort into a tumbler, tossed it down his throat, bared his teeth. I saw the gap where a molar had recently been removed.

The crowd were pussy-footing about, draping coats on backs of chairs, making idle chit-chat. I shook the man with the muddy browns off, beat a path through the bodies towards Mum. She fussed with Granny Bee, settled her into a booth. By the vacant look of Vera, she was revisiting past events. Big Shirley seemed as nervous as a nun in a brothel. I wondered what would happen next, didn't wait long to find out, courtesy of Dad. He bellowed. Anger with no place to go wrapped around his words.

"Come on then, you lot, drinks are on the house. Make the most of it 'cos you'll not set a bleeding foot in here again, not as long as I live you won't."

I detected apprehension in the air. Faces checked others out, communicated with raised eyebrows, grimaces. The man with the muddy browns slipped behind the bar, pulled a few pints, sat them on the cherry wood.

"Oh buggerations," Big Shirley said. "What did I tell you, Joanie? Didn't I say he'd start on the melodramatics?"

"Well, it's best he gets it out of his system, Shirley," Mum said.

"Might be best for him, but I think he means it, Joan, I think it's the end of the line for The Bee Hive. Christ, after all these years an' all. This club's been through a war, you know."

"I'm hardly likely to forget that, am I, Shirley? Trouble is, it's not been through something like this, has it?"

I understood that to mean murder, 'cos though it hadn't been said in so many words, that's what it boiled down to. Cold blooded murder. After all, I'd seen the gun, heard the threat. And now Black Jack was on the run. It didn't take a genius to work it out, did it?

"But what'll I do, Joan?" Big Shirley slumped against the upholstery, the fight knocked out of her. "Where will I go?"

"Oh Shirley, I don't know." Mum closed a hand over hers. "I just don't know."

I squeezed myself in beside Vera. The five of us sat with our hang-dogs on. Most others began the business of drinking the club dry. I began the business of making a fool proof plan, one that involved me hearing things I shouldn't hear.

"Don't look now, Joanie." Big Shirley muttered out the west side of her mouth, nodded her head east. "But you should see what the bloody cat's dragged in."

Naturally, Mum looked at what the bloody cat dragged in. Naturally, I felt obligated to do likewise, executed a sideslip to gain a clearer view. A wafer thin woman had paused in the doorway. Her hair was shocking red, too long considering the years she carried. Somehow it suited her. She shrugged off a silver grey fur coat, draped it over a shoulder. Underneath she wore a royal blue blouse, tailored black trousers, was taller than most men. Her legs almost reached her armpits.

"Oh, it's her." Mum's eyes glittered. She tightened her grip on the brandy glass. I noticed her knuckles turn white.

My peepers travelled back to the red head. They watched her glide forward on those lengthy pins. Dad watched her too.

"Who's she?" I said to nobody in particular.

"Rita Swan, that's who she is." Big Shirley sniffed, added a sneer. "Failed actress and general no-gooder."

"Nothing but a trollop," Mum said. "That's what she is."

Rita Swan reached the bar, slipped onto a stool, shook a filter tip from a gold case.

"Give me a double, Mickey," she said. "And a light, if you don't mind."

Dad scraped a match, held it to the filter tip. She dragged in deep, blew smoke to heaven.

"What'll you have, Rita?" I heard a certain tension in his tone, paid extra attention to the goings-on between them.

"You know what I'm partial to, Mickey." She flapped thick lashes at him. I had a feeling she wasn't only talking about the drink. Dad poured whiskey, added a splash of soda, offered up the tumbler. Her fingers wrapped his hand, held it prisoner. She raised the glass, sipped, smiled the sort of smile I imagined only lovers shared. Dad didn't send one in return.

"I could slap her into next week, I could," Big Shirley said.

"She's not worth making a scene over," Mum said.

I heard the jukebox whirl. A record dropped. The stylus crackled as it touched on the 45. Little Richard screamed for Lucille. He wanted her back where she belonged. I wondered if she wanted that too, wondered why she took off in the first place. She must have had her reasons.

Rita Swan gathered the whiskey bottle, tumbler, the rest of her paraphernalia, made headway towards an empty table for two near the double front doors.

"Hey, Rita," a male voice said. "Want some company to go with that bottle?"

"Not yours I don't." She flicked her hair, continued on without as much as a break in her stride.

That's the moment the plan pulled itself together. Call it intuition, or even a plain and simple hunch, but I was as certain as hell is hot Rita Swan, the no-gooder, was my ticket to the past nobody else would share. I just needed to judge when the time was right, when the hard stuff had hit the soft spot that liberates loose talk, when my parents relaxed their eagle eyes. And that's what I did.

The clock nudged eleven. Mum decided Granny Bee should retire. Dad was well and truly oiled. The fag smoke was practically thick enough to float on. I started roaming the room, lingered here and there, earwigged on a few slurred conversations, learned some poor girl was knocked up out of wedlock, another had caught her cheating boyfriend with his pants down. I worked half a dozen tables before moving in on Rita Swan. Another filter tip dangled from the corner of her painted mouth. The left eye squinted, the right encouraged me over. I inched closer.

"Come and join me," she said. "Or have you been warned off?"

I gave her my bored expression, backed it with a sigh.

"I pretty much do what I want," I said.

"Me too." She indulged in a shot of nicotine. "So, what do you want to know?"

"I want to know everything."

"Then you better take a seat." A smug curve tugged at her lips. "I know plenty. It could take quite a while."

8

I toyed **with the** idea of leaving Rita Swan high and dry, but as I'm a
nosy little tyke, toying was as far as it got. Trying not to appear over
eager, I casually sat, took a lazy look-see around the club. Denny
was hitting on a tawny haired girl. He leaned west, whispered in her ear.
She pretended to be shocked, slapped his hand, shook her head. Her eyes
were saying something entirely different though, something like maybe. He
followed it up with a neck nuzzle. I witnessed the something like maybe melt
into a sure fire definite. The girl was done for. Another poor cow had been
outwitted.

I turned my focus towards the bar. Sullivan propped up the cherry wood,
bottle of Coke in hand. Apart from myself, he was the only other teetotaller
in the room. I gave him the once over, noticed his shoes were heavy Doc
Martens. My peepers drifted north, met the muddy browns. I still saw danger.
He still saw everything. That's the problem with me, my face doesn't lie even
when my tongue reels them off.

He smiled that crooked smile again. I sent a cautious one back. A petite
strawberry blonde joined him, hijacked his attention. Her left palm pressed
her belly, the right fluttered towards her heart. She scuttled into the circle
of his arms, laid her cheek against his chest. A single tear pooled in her
eye, trickled across the curve of her cheek. I heard him say, "Oh, Stella,"
wondered if they were an item.

"So, Ruby Blackbee, I suppose you've worked out things aren't as
straight as you thought they were," Rita said, "especially where your father's
concerned."

My concentration returned to the matter in hand, pretty darn quick, in
fact. Billy Fury began griping about his girl leaving him halfway to paradise.
I assumed she was holding on to her assets.

"What do you mean my Dad's not as straight as I thought?" I curled a lip,
Elvis style.

Rita traced the rim of the tumbler with a red lacquered fingernail, rocked her head to the side, slipped me a crafty look. Instinct told me I was about to hear some very unsavoury secrets. I could hardly bear the wait, though it would be distasteful to learn that someone you held in the highest esteem walked on the wrong side of the track, wouldn't it?

"You know bugger all, don't you," she said through a smirk. "I bet you don't even know your Dad used to be a bare knuckle fighter."

Of course I didn't know Dad used to be a bare knuckle fighter. How could I with parents who made the habit of hiding secrets they had no business hiding. I heaved a shoulder, let it drop.

"Well he was, would have been as famous as Freddie Mills if it weren't for your Grampy George. Surely you've heard of the wrong-doings of that old goat, God rest his soul."

Of course I knew less than nothing of the wrong-doings of that old goat, God rest his soul. I scraped the chair nearer to Rita's, leaned towards her. Our faces were inches apart, close enough for me to count the pores on her skin, smell her perfume, something classy, maybe Chanel.

"What about the old goat?" I said.

"He made lives a misery, that's what. The meanest man I ever had the misfortune to meet, hated Stavros with a vengeance, and we all know why that was, don't we?"

I took a minute to go muck raking through my memories, recalled a speculation I once earwigged on, about the disappearance of a Greek sailor who'd wormed his way into Granny Bee's affections. My thinking did a bit of overtime, came up trumps with another secret.

"Are you saying the Greek sailor had something to do with it?" I said.

Rita threw her head backwards, laughed open-mouthed. Her teeth were nicotine stained, her breath smelled of whiskey and smoke.

"I'm saying the Greek sailor had a lot to do with it," she said.

I leaned in further. She met me halfway. I noticed her eyes were sea green flecked with gold. I hated to ask the next question, 'cos I already knew the answer.

"Are you saying Granny Bee had an affair?" I said.

"I'm saying it's common knowledge the Blackbee boys weren't full blood brothers, and Grampy George made his wife pay every single day he had left on earth, that he did. Oh yes, Molly paid her dues, one way or the other."

I eased myself back, peeled my peepers off hers, fixed them on the man with skin criss-crossed by wrinkles at a neighbouring table. I caught a faint aroma of the trusty TCP.

He unwrapped a cigarillo, clamped it between his lips, struck a match, gave it the brush of fire, coughed his lungs up. My peepers made a reluctant return to Rita's.

"I don't believe you," I said.

"Makes no difference to me what you believe." She shrugged, poured a tot of whiskey.

"You'll just never know why George was the meanest man I ever met, or how he died." She nodded towards Vera, holed up in the booth with a bottle of vodka. "You'll never know about her, either, and what makes her the saddest drunk there ever was." She paused, sipped the devils brew, wiped the lipstick smear of the tumbler with the pad of her thumb. "And you'll certainly never know where Black Jack fits into all this mess, will you?"

Rita Swan smiled a sweet smile of complete confidence. She was as sure as rain was wet that last little gem would bring me back on side. And she was right. Nevertheless, I took the vow of silence for a few seconds, prepared my heart for another bruising before I said, "Tell me about Black Jack."

"Shall we start at the beginning?" She settled herself on the chair, crossed one long leg over the other, offered me a Woodbine. I declined. She offered a drop of devil's brew. I declined that, too. "You've heard George was a sniper in the Great War, haven't you?"

"What? A sniper?" I said. "That's cold blooded murder, that is."

"That's war. You're lucky; you've not lived through a war, have you? What can you possibly know?"

Well, she clean had me there, didn't she? Besides, it's hard to argue with the truth, so I didn't, just listened as she set off on a detour down memory lane. To be honest, I could have done without the detour. The club was thinning out. Several folk had already wobbled their way into the street. Others were tussling with their coats. Without the crowd for camouflage, Dad would soon clock me sat at the table for two with Rita Swan, would pack me off to bed like the kid he still thought I was.

"And so George returned a flawed man," Rita said. "It didn't show; it was all up here." She tapped her head with the index finger on her left hand. I recalled Steven Shaw patrolling the garden fence at home, another flawed soldier from another war. "Took to the mother's ruin like a duck takes to water."

Rita's eyes glazed. The devil's brew was taking her under. I started to worry she'd never get to the part where Black Jack fitted into the mess. I noticed Dad move out from behind the cherry wood, noticed the TCP man greet him with a handshake.

"What's the mother's ruin got to do with anything?" I said.

"It got him killed, that's what," she said.

My peepers swerved west to Rita's. Hers were on Dad.

"What d'ya mean, got him killed?"

"It happened late one evening."

I waited for more. Whilst waiting, I watched the TCP man lift his puny fists. Dad accepted the challenge. They did a bit of the old one-two. Dad pretended to stagger from an uppercut. They laughed, hugged. For the shortest of moments, regrets showed on both their faces. I gave a lengthy sigh, had the suspicion I'd soon be reaping in some regrets of my own.

"What happened late one evening?" I said.

"The fight happened," she said. "I shouldn't have even been there."

I waited again. She rummaged in her handbag, pulled out a hankie, blotted her eyes. That's the trouble with the partaking of intoxicating liquor, it tends to bring on a fit of the maudlins. I sighed again.

"Then why were you there, Rita?" I said.

"Because I was the driver, that's why. There were four of us, me, your Dad, Jack and Abraham Golding. That's him over there." She tipped her head at the TCP man. "He was the go-between, the tallyman, the trainer, manager and God knows what else. Kept the cops greased an' all with some nice little backhanders. A lot of money was made. It's how your Dad got this place."

I was reluctant to stop her now she'd finally got going, but she'd raised the subject of the Bee Hive's ownership, the one I thought belonged to Uncle Stavros. I held up the flat of my palm, said, "Hold your horses. Let me get this straight. Are you saying my Dad is the legal owner of this poxy run-down flea pit?"

"Of course your Dad is the legal owner of this poxy run-down flea pit." Her face made a frown. Her pencilled-on eyebrows met over the bridge of her nose. Behind her eyes I saw her putting two and two together. She barked out a laugh, looked as happy as a dog with a street full of lamp posts. "Oh dear me, you really have been kept in the dark, haven't you?"

As I'd practically exhausted my reserve of sighs, I curled my top lip, offered Rita a snarl instead. A growl rumbled in my throat. I was close to inflicting some bodily harm upon her. In need of extra fortification I helped myself to a swig of devil's brew. It burned a path through my innards right down to my toes. When I could speak again, I said, "Just tell me what happened."

Rita Swan gave it to me with no frills.

"Your Dad won another fight," she said, "a big earner. He was going places, and we were going with him, all the way to the top. I drove them home, got persuaded to join in with a victory nightcap. Only we found George in a drunken rage, tearing the club apart, smashing chairs, up-ending tables. Granny Bee and Stavros were cowering behind the bar. Stavros must have taken a hit. He was holding a hanky to his eye. It was soaked in blood. Well, there was precious little chance the great Mickey Blackbee would stand by and watch everything he'd worked for get smashed to smithereens, that's for sure." She broke off, lit a gasper. I detected a trace of bitterness in her tone. "In he waded, hustling George against the wall. Jack tried to get between them, tried to calm things down. But George was beyond reasoning. He took a punch, missed by a mile. Your Dad laughed in his face. I heard utter loathing in that laugh the like I've never heard before, or since. And then, as God is my witness, George just buckled, gasping for breath. I remember screaming. I remember your Dad telling us to get Granny Bee away, he'd deal with it. We didn't argue. We went upstairs. I kept watch at the window for the ambulance. Abraham tended to Stavros. Jack comforted Granny Bee. She said all he needed was his heart pill, he'd be right as rain once he had that, he always was."

Rita paused again, dropped a hand showing signs of age upon mine. It felt cold. I slid mine out from under hers. She narrowed her sea greens, coiled her fingers around the tumbler of devils brew. "All I know is the ambulance never came, and George wasn't as right as rain. No-one spoke about that night ever again, but I think we all knew …"

I didn't get to hear what they all thought they knew. A shadow spread itself over the table. Rita snapped her mouth shut. I caught a glimpse of Big Shirley out of the corner of my left eye. She hoisted me off the chair by the scruff of my neck without so much as an excuse me please, strong-armed me across the parquet dance floor, along the bar, through the heavy duty doors, up the flight of stairs into a kitchen that smelled of lemons. The sound of jeering followed us. I can assure you, I struggled every step of the way. As soon as her grip loosened, I turned, prepared to do battle. I wasn't going down without a fight.

"Raised a proper little firecracker here, haven't you, Joanie?" Big Shirley said.

Pulling myself up to my full five foot two height, I pinned her with a filthy look.

"What's she been up to now?"

My peepers swivelled east in their sockets towards the familiar voice of long suffering.

I noticed the bare brick archway, noticed Mum move away from a dark wood table. She sounded less than pleased to see me. To her right, Granny Bee sat on a carver, a large marmalade cat curled upon her lap. It cracked one amber eye apart, observed the disturbance, shifted position. She stroked it back to sleep.

"Nothing, she's been as quiet as a lamb."

Big Shirley gave me a long, hard look. I gave her one back. She broke first, strolled to the cooker, lit the gas, slid the whistler over the flame. It flattened out. Yellow flares licked around the base. She leaned a hip against a beech worktop, resumed eye contact. I felt obligated to do likewise.

"I find that almost impossible to believe, Shirley." Mum joined me, wrapped her arm around my shoulders. I pressed myself against the softness of her. "Are you alright, Ruby?"

"Of course she's alright."

Big Shirley answered on my behalf, gave me a wink. It was a relief not to be forced to tell another fib. Even though I didn't want to, I felt something like gratitude towards her.

"Well, it's been quite a day, hasn't it? I think we best get some shut-eye. Could you show Ruby to Mickey's bedroom, Shirley? I'll get Granny Bee into her pit then pop up and say nighty-night."

"Let's go, squirt." Big Shirley took my hand, led me to a staircase just wide enough for one hidden behind a white glossed door. She flicked a switch, waved me forward. I hesitated for a second, then started to climb. My silhouette escorted me. "These old buildings are full of surprises, aren't they? Cubby holes where you least expect them. Rumour has it, this used to be a brothel way back when."

I said nothing as loud as I could; waited on the square landing for her to catch up. The heels proved a hindrance. The pencil skirt didn't help either.

"I've put your case in here." She pushed the door open on my west side. The glow from a bedside lamp beckoned me forward. "Used to be your Dad's. I'm kipping next door, your Uncle's room."

A chill slid down my spine. I wondered if his belongings were still in situ, wondered if his pillow still smelled of his cologne, if his slippers were still on the floor. I wondered if Big Shirley would get any sleep. She must have been wondering the same.

"I hope he doesn't feel inclined to pay a little visit." She smiled a smile bordering on sickly. "Else I'll be gone from here faster than a sailor on a four hour pass."

I dredged up a sneer, took my tired body into the bedroom, left her standing on the landing. It was a while before I heard Uncle Stavros' door close. It started to rain. The drops beat out a drum roll on the roof. I looked around. There wasn't much to see, a single bed, a combination wardrobe, an overstuffed chair. I pulled out my pink flannelette pyjamas, got ready to retire, lifted the bedclothes, eased myself between cotton sheets. A hot water bottle welcomed me in. I heard Mum on the stairs; shut my eyelids down tight, faked sleep.

She turned out the bedside lamp, smoothed the hair from my brow, replaced it with a kiss.

Luckily, she left the door ajar. The landing light threw an orange glow against the curtains, which was just as well, 'cos me and the dark aren't in perfect harmony.

My lugholes picked up the sound of floorboards complaining, the sound of whispers. I eased myself out of bed, tippy-toed to the door for an earwigging, couldn't catch a single clear word. I positioned a peeper to spy on the goings-on taking place. Well, my lower jaw fell that fast it almost suffered a fracture. Now it all made perfect sense. Big Shirley was a man.

9

I woke to the tune of woodpeckers drilling on wood. For a few precious seconds I dozed in the half dark without a single thought to worry about. But soon enough, yesterday's tragedy put paid to the peace. I remembered where I was, and why. Naturally, once they started, the thoughts came thick and fast. It was still all a dirty rotten shame. Uncle Stavros was still pushing up daisies. I still knew nothing worth knowing. How much more would Rita Swan have told if Big Shirley hadn't strong-armed me away? Where did that murdering scumbag Black Jack fit in? What lay behind the secret door in the hall? Why was Vodka Vera the saddest drunk there ever was. And most disturbing of all, did Dad let Grampy George die?

I heard the whistling of *Carolina Moon* grow louder, split an eyelid. Although the morning hadn't yet fully lit the day, I recognised Dad's shape loitering in the doorway.

"Rise and shine, Ruby darlin'."

He circled the space between bed and window. My peeper circled with him. He knelt beside the bed, fixed me with a look, the no-nonsense one he was inclined to use when he felt cranky. The faint smell of fresh mint toothpaste fanned the foot or so that separated us, tried its best to disguise last night's whiskey breath.

I propped myself up on an elbow. Dad reversed an inch. I duly noticed he was suffering the side effects of a heavy night. His bloodshot eyes were underlined with blue smudges. I could almost see his brain throbbing in his skull. That warned me his patience had grown thin before I could set about testing it. I would need to choose my words carefully.

"What's going on, Dad?" I said.

"What do you mean, what's going on?" he said.

The gang of woodpeckers outside upped their efforts. Dad muttered a curse, pushed himself vertical, strode to the window, flung it wide. Cold air hurried in. I tugged the lemon candlewick bedspread over my shoulders.

"Sullivan, give that bloody hammer a rest, will you? Jeez, the sooner I put some miles between me and this damn place the better."

He returned bedside. We spent time sizing each other up.

"Now, get ready for the off, Ruby, or stay here. I'm not bothered either way, but your mother might be."

I put as much ill-will into a huff that I could. As usual he skirted round my questions, like he always did when there were unspeakable things to learn. Unfortunately for him, I'm a human bloodhound once I pick up the scent of a secret.

"So what's going on, Dad?" I said.

"About what?" Irritation edged his voice.

"Well, Big Shirley for a start. She's not a proper woman, is she?"

"That old queen? She's a drag act, darlin', just doesn't know where to draw the line. Should have kicked her out years ago, she's a bleeding liability."

He made for the door. His hand reached for the handle. In a few seconds he'd be gone.

I should have let him go, should have left the past where it belonged. But that's the problem with me, I can't leave other people's business alone.

"Rita Swan said you used to be a boxer." I sat straighter, put on my martyr's expression. "Why don't I know about that? What's the big secret?"

I heard the sound of a long sigh, waited for his reply. Whilst waiting I studied his profile. He still looked like my dad, the same sharp nose, the dark eyebrows, the short back and sides he had tidied at Benny's every six weeks. But his grey eyes had lost something. Vera once said they're the windows of our soul. I reckon she's right. Just before he pulled himself together I clearly saw his soul in torment that morning. In that short unguarded moment, I knew, without a doubt, he'd never get over the loss of Uncle Stavros, even if it was true they weren't full blood brothers.

"There's no big secret, darlin'." Dad took from his trousers pocket a tin of Sun Valley, a pack of blue Rizlas. "I did a bit of boxing, and now I don't."

"Rita Swan said Grampy George was the meanest man she'd ever had the misfortune to meet."

"Yep, he was." He rolled a choker one-handed, tucked it between his lips, searched out his silver Zippo lighter. "And afterwards nobody missed him, he was that mean."

"But you tried to help him, didn't you, Dad?" I felt my ticker pick up speed, placed a palm over it. "You gave him the heart pill, didn't you, the one that always made him right as rain?"

He kept his peepers on mine as he lit up, dragged hard on the choker.

His cheeks collapsed like a pair of squeezed bellows. I noticed he hadn't de-whiskered, noticed his shirt was crumpled. I doubted he'd found his way to bed after the last mourner had finally bid adios. Maybe he slept where he fell. Maybe he hadn't slept at all.

"Hey, what's this all about, darlin'?" he said.

"It's about the truth." I stabbed him with a look loaded with more bravado than common sense.

"The truth, eh? I'll give you the truth, my girl, and then we'll talk of it no more. Your granddad was past help, had been for years. And that's the God's honest." He slipped from the room to the landing. "Get packed, I'm leaving in fifteen minutes."

"What about The Bee Hive?" I said.

"It's closed." I heard his shoes hit the stairs.

"What about Big Shirley, and Granny Bee? What about them, Dad?"

"Big Shirley can care for herself. Granny Bee's coming with us."

I was out of bed faster than a whippet springs from the trap, raced to the landing. Dad had already reached the bottom of the staircase just wide enough for one.

"What do you mean, coming with us?"

He turned. For a few seconds we sized each other up like a couple of gunslingers do, him in his crumpled shirt, me in pink flannelette pyjamas.

"She can't stay on her ownsome, can she?" he said.

"Why should we have her?"

"Because we're all she's got left."

"But I don't get on with her." I heard my voice whine.

"I hate to break the bad news, darlin', but as it happens, she don't think much of you either, says you're a spoilt brat. You've only got ten minutes now, and don't make me come fetch you, Ruby Blackbee, else I'll have your guts for garters, you hear?"

I heard him loud and clear, made it to the kitchen in eight minutes flat. The spare two I spent wisely, glaring at the quiet gathering round the table. Granny Bee was good to go, black coat buttoned, handbag at the ready. A gold coloured wicker basket sat at her feet. It creaked as the marmalade cat performed a couple of tight spins. So he was in on the raid too.

"Where's my boy?" Granny Bee said.

I detected a stiffening of spines, a thinning of lips. We all knew she was asking after Uncle Stavros. When nobody rushed to reply, I opened my mouth, took a breath. There was no easy way to tell her where her boy was. I decided honesty was the best policy. For my efforts Big Shirley elbowed me in the ribcage, shot me a look loaded with daggers. I fired one back, bared my teeth the way the Shaw brothers mongrel does when you try to whip the butcher's bone off him. During the moments of our unspoken exchange I noticed her attire. She'd opted for a forties flavour that morning, floor sweeping periwinkle gown, star spangled mules, a chestnut wig styled in soft waves, understated make-up. I definitely saw a loose resemblance to Lauren Bacall.

"He's not here, Duchess," Mum said.

"Okay, let's rock 'n' roll," Dad said. "The Doyles are outside already."

We collected our belongings, single filed onto the street. I recall a dove grey sky, a breeze cold enough to cut clean through to the bone. I shrank further into my coat, took a nosy around. The Club windows were blinded with brown chipboard. A claw hammer swung from Sullivan's right hand. Denny's motorbike spluttered. He gave it extra revs. Mr Doyle cocked his leg over the pillion seat, swayed to the left. A pot-bellied man stood in the open doorway of Stan's Greasy Spoon. I assumed it was Stan himself. An off-white apron tied round his middle gave me the clue. Dad nodded in his direction. Pot-Belly nodded back. Several chins rippled. He linked fat fingers over his generous girth.

I sat between Granny Bee and Vera in the back of the Ford Cortina. Mum hugged Big Shirley, took her place upfront. The cat rode in the boot hemmed in by luggage.

"Wagons roll," Dad said.

We began the journey home. As we rolled I took a last look-see at the Club. Sullivan stood on his lonesome. He lifted a hand, saluted. I saluted too. Granny Bee started up singing about ten green bottles. Her voice was surprisingly tuneful. Nobody else felt the urge to join her in song. She reached the end, asked how much further we had to go.

"Miles," Dad said.

"Bloody hell's bells," she said. "So, Joanie, what did you and Rita have a two and eight about last night?"

Well, I'm sure you'll understand perfectly how that question set my lugholes flapping.

I tipped forward, filled the gap separating the front seats, noticed Mum cast her eyes to the ether.

"Just a difference of opinion," she said.

"Sounded more like you had a touch of the green-eyed monster," Granny

Bee said. "Jealousy's not at all attractive in a woman, you know, only makes her look cheap."

"Don't be ridiculous, Duchess, I'm much too old to be bothered with jealousy."

"Maybe you should be bothered, Joan. Even now Rita would take my Mickey on, though why she's still interested beats me. He's weighed down with enough baggage to sink a battleship."

"Thanks very much," Dad said.

"But don't you ever sometimes wonder, son, what might have been?" She delved into her handbag, found a packet of Polos, slipped one through her thin lips. "Rita Swan's loaded, you could have been somebody tucked up with her."

"I am somebody," Dad said.

"And as for my boy." She gave a lusty sigh. I felt the heat of hot air on the back of my neck, smelled the aroma of peppermint. "Unlucky in love, that's him. I always thought he was rather sweet on you, Joanie. Perhaps you married the wrong brother."

I noticed Dad's hands tighten on the steering wheel. His knuckles were white tipped.

Mum drummed fingers against her knee. It was a sure giveaway she was close to blowing a gasket. I turned, raised my eyebrows, gave Granny Bee an enquiring look. She gave me a hostile one back.

"Anyway, you can't undo what's done, can you?" she said. "But I wish I knew where my boy's gone. He's always disappearing lately. He could have at least left me a note. He knows how I worry."

"He left a bloody note all right," Dad said.

"Mickey, don't." Mum placed a hand on his knee, swivelled her head, looked Granny Bee straight in the eye. "That's why you're staying with us, Duchess, until things get sorted. It'll be a little holiday for you."

"Oh that's nice, Joan, but only til my boy comes to take me home, eh."

"Yes, only til then."

It's fair to say that short exchange put a damper on my immediate future. Uncle Stavros was never coming to take Granny Bee home. He was planted six feet under, wasn't he? It would truly be the miracle of the century if he came gunning southwards in his fancy car, decked out in a Carnaby Street suit, gold tooth flashing, with trouble as usual following hot on his heels. We were lumbered with her forever, and not just with her in person. She was bringing with her the scent of lavender, the slurping of tea, a tongue as sharp as a cut-throat razor, aggravation, arguments, the sodding marmalade cat. And that was just for starters.

"So how far did you say it was, Mickey?" she said. "Can't keep Monty cooped up in that basket for too long, you know."

"Miles," Dad said.

"Bloody hell's bells."

It was then a lack of charity hitched a lift on my sense of justice. If it were fate someone had to have their brains blown out, why couldn't it have been her?

10

I wish I could tell you that Uncle Stavros' demise pulled us together like only a tragedy can.

But it didn't. We were almost reluctant to mention his name, almost fearful that to do so would knock the scabs off our wounded hearts. And when those scabs on my heart sometimes itched I refused to scratch them, 'cos no word of a lie, if I did, the chances were I'd slowly bleed to death.

Granny Bee fared better than the rest of us, probably due to the fact she was a few bob short of a pound. She made herself comfy in the big back bedroom, which used to be mine, quicker than a flea on a stray dog. On the well-oiled Singer, Mum ran up a pink flower print bedspread, matching curtains, loose covers for the threadbare easy chair. Dad acquired an antique radiogram she was familiar with. I gallantly suffered through endless playing of crackly '78s, foot tapped along to Glen Miller, learned by repetition songs by Gracie Fields, The Andrew Sisters, grew quite fond of the boogie-woogie bugle boy of Company B.

She even joined the tea and talk brigade round our kitchen table, paid visits to the Shaw brothers next door, reliving the war over a bottle of Harvey's Bristol Cream. Mostly though she annoyed me. As I'm not the shy retiring type, a verbal ding-dong usually flared. In a strange way we rather enjoyed the clearing of grievances. In retrospect I can see it was the only thing we had in common. Not much is it?

Anyway, we'd go for it hammer and tongs till Mum broke up the barney. Then she'd try her hardest to reason with my conscience, the one I kept hidden when it suited.

"Must you bicker with your Granny every second of the blinking day, Ruby? Can't you at least try to be nice before I'm forced to slap you both into next Sunday?"

With fingers crossed behind my back I promised to at least try. Of course any fool knows fingers crossed cancels out a promise, but I did try the once. Granny Bee had been holed up in our house for five months. It looked a dead cert she was here for the duration. I felt the urge to rake over the past again. I rapped my knuckles on the bedroom door, entered without an invite, waited for her to make the first move. She finished a row of knitting, laid it on her lap. The scent of lavender jostled with the smell of moth-eaten cat.

"Back for annihilation, are you?" she said.

"If I'm going down I'll take you with me, you can bet your bottom dollar on that" I said.

"So what do you want to argue about this time, eh? Got anything particular in mind?"

I jiggled a few ideas around. It was comforting to find several budding arguments festering. I showed admirable restraint not to rise to the bait. After all, I needed her to look back in time, something she was exceptionally good at doing. It was living in the present she had problems with.

"Nothing in particular at the moment," I said, "just wondered if you fancy a cup of splosh."

Her peepers slimmed, her brow furrowed. I sliced my lips into a smirk.

"A cup of splosh? You plotting some kind of skulduggery, trying to get one over on me, of all people? I'll have you know I'm too sharp to fall for any of your tricks, girl."

"Bloody hell." I buttered my voice thick with righteous anger. "Can't even ask if you want a cuppa now, can I?"

"Not without an ulterior motive, you can't." She crossed her arms, hoisted her bosoms north. "Still crabby about this bedroom, aren't you? Still got the hump 'cos you've been demoted to the box-room, I suppose. Well, it's no use whining over lost battles, and I can't be bothered, so, if you'll excuse me, I'm busy knitting a balaclava for Steven, for his undercover mission. It's top secret, you know, and I'll say no more. Don't forget, walls have ears."

She picked up the needles, started click-clacking. A yellow silk scarf loosely circled her neck. If I yanked it tight I wondered how long it would take to polish her off, if she'd struggle much.

I forced myself to turn away. On the windowsill Monty the marmalade cat soaked up the rays, glared at me for interrupting his afternoon siesta. His eyes were the colour of butterscotch. They plainly showed utter contempt. I hummed a growl. He hurled a hiss. I returned my attention to Granny Bee again. She'd touched on a nerve bringing the bedroom battle back into play.

"Actually, I think you'll find the bedroom battle was a draw," I said.

For the second time she laid her knitting down, studied me with shrewd peepers. I noted they were grey, same as Dad's. I carefully kept mine blank.

"A draw you say?" One of her pencilled on eyebrows arched dramatically.

"Yes," I said.

"How do you work that out then, girl?"

"Well." I sat on the foot of her queen size bed. A smirk stretched my lips.

"Don't get too comfy, will you," she said. "I don't intend putting up with your company any longer than necessary."

I toed off my shoes, tucked legs beneath my derriere, caught a shadow of annoyance cross her face before she had the chance to replace it with a stare. The smirk stretched wider.

"It may have been my bedroom before you took on squatters rights," I said, "but truth be told I didn't mind moving that much, not really."

"Rubbish." She snorted like the rag and bone man's old nag. "You threw a tantrum any two year old would be proud of."

"Of course I did." I unfurled my legs, slipped on shoes, resumed standing position.

"It's what's expected of me, isn't it? So, do you want that tea or not?"

We gave one another the once over, me still wearing the smirk, her with suspicion still in place.

"And risk you spitting in it? Not bloody likely." I heard the stirrings of a laugh begin in her scraggy throat. "Oh you're a sly one, Ruby Blackbee, no doubt about that."

Monty took the stirrings of a laugh as a peace treaty, stretched, sauntered over to weave around my legs. Cats do that sort of thing. They're either leg weavers or head butters. Monty was a leg man.

Granny Bee leaned westwards, plucked a small blue glass bottle off the bedside cabinet, unscrewed the cap, sniffed in the contents.

"That's better," she said. "Nothing beats a sniff of the smelling salts to clear the head."

She offered the bottle my way. "Care to participate in the salts, girl?"

I heard the hint of a challenge in her voice, reached for the bottle, could already whiff something unsavoury from an arm's length away, wished I'd had the good sense to decline.

Unfortunately, by accepting the bottle I'd gone too far, didn't want to listen to her gloating I had no guts, 'cos I knew she would.

"Go on then, if you've got the guts."

I sighed; made sure I indulged in a decent sniff. The salts exploded in the nostrils. My peepers bulged, filled to overflowing with tears. I staggered a few steps, thought I might be close to passing out. The echo of a belly buster brought me round.

"Well, you don't do things by half measures, do you girl. I'll give you that much," Granny Bee said. "That's made my day that has. Your face was a right picture."

"So it's agreed, is it?" I knuckled the tears dry. "The bedroom battle is a draw."

She clucked her tongue, replaced the bottle cap, returned it to the bedside cabinet, gave me a considering look.

"Luckily you've caught me in a generous mood," she said. "But I can afford to be, can't I, seeing as the score is six-three to me. Got some catching up to do, girl, haven't you?"

It's only fair to confess I took full advantage of Granny Bee's generous mood, wouldn't want to mislead anyone into believing we miraculously began to rub nicely along. The young are like that. Half are goody two shoes, the other mercenary little maggots. I fall into the latter category. Personally I'd rather be like Grace. Even though we weren't old enough, she had her future mapped out. It included JJ Duffy, marriage, babies, happy ever after. She already had Duffy dancing to her tune. No doubt the babies would come nine months after that band of gold was on her finger. Or maybe before if they gave way to temptation. Only fate could decide the happy ever after, and everybody knows it doesn't always play fair, does it?

As for me, making life simple just wasn't in my nature. That's why I loved a boy who was no good, who even put the voodoos on all my future boy liasons. Denny Doyle ruined me. And I let him. And I let my thirst for the truth winkle out a secret that was best left unwinkled too. The day I sweet talked Granny Bee into looking back in time was the day I started reaping the regrets.

"I'll catch up, Granny Bee, don't you worry about that." I re-fixed the smirk over my face.

"Now what are you smirking like some halfwit for, girl?" she said.

"No reason," I said. "I was thinking, stuck down here in the south, you must be missing all your old friends in Soho. You must be lonely sometimes."

"All my old friends have long gone." She gave a feeble sigh. I noticed her eyes had a faraway look about them, "The friends that count, that is. Besides, Soho isn't what it used to be anymore. The streets are packed with bums and half naked girls nowadays. Bloody place has gone to rack and ruin."

I gave a lusty sigh, walked to the window, inspected the scenery. It was mid July, the garden was at its best. Roses were bursting, their scent strong on the breeze. The sun had singed the lawn. Yellow patches spotted the green. No doubt, come evening, Mum would turn the hose on it. Next door, the Shaw brothers' dog snoozed in the shade of a purple fuchsia bush. Now and then his paws twitched. I wondered if he was dreaming.

"Tell me about all your long gone old friends, Granny Bee." I turned my head left, watched Grace and Duffy canoodling on the swing seat Mr Doyle found ditched in the spinney. It hadn't taken much to mend, a couple of slats, a lick of gloss. I decided to join them once I'd squeezed the secrets out of Granny Bee. Grace wouldn't mind me playing gooseberry. Like she used to say, boys come and go; friends are forever. Of course that was prior to Duffy arriving on the scene offering his undying love and devotion.

I listened with lugholes half cocked as Granny Bee talked of her childhood pal, Prudence Wright, who gave herself to God, travelled to far flung lands preaching the gospel, returned to nurse injured soldiers during the Great War, only to perish in the blitz of '43 whilst queuing for a black market tin of Spam . I heard about Trinidad Belle, a dusky beauty, taken in by Gus Adams, the well respected grocer. They never married but she bore him a son anyway, named him Jack.

"Hang on." I halted her with an open palm. My heartbeat broke into a gallop. "Is that the same Jack as Dad's army buddy? "

"Who else would it be? Grew up side by side, those two did, got into all sorts of mischief an' all, then marched off to war thinking they were heroes already, bloody fools."

Granny Bee smoothed her dress down, patted her knees. Monty accepted the summons, took up residence on her lap, began purring. "Hardly ever wrote home, selfish, the pair of them. And then they got a fortnights leave, came back with your mother in tow, and Jack met Vera, a recipe for disaster in the making that was." She tipped her chin south, ran her hand along Monty's fur coat. "And then the Bethnal Green tragedy happened."

I rolled the information around, latched onto a couple of words that seemed to slip together like lovers do, Jack and Vera. It was the perfect lead for a bit of cross-examination.

I moved nearer to Granny Bee, knelt in front of her. My lips were burning with questions. Monty gave me a warning rumble. I backed off.

"Granny Bee, what happened at Bethnal Green?" I said.

She didn't answer. I leaned closer, raised my face, noticed she was deep-rooted in a memory so distressing it had drained the blood from her press powdered cheeks.

"What do you mean, what happened at Bethnal Green?" Her eyelids fluttered shut. They were as creased as an un-ironed shirt. "Don't you remember?"

I groaned. Obviously Granny Bee had lost touch with the here and now. I wouldn't be learning the secret of Jack and the tragedy at Bethnal Green anytime soon. I heard the front doorbell chime a jingle. It was new. I don't know where Dad got it from but I wished he hadn't bothered. Now we had the opening bars of God Save the Queen every time a caller came calling. It rang again. Granny Bee's eyelids rolled up. We stared at one another for a number of seconds.

"Someone's at the door." She turfed Monty off her knee. He re-occupied his position on the windowsill. I skedaddled down the stairs, opened the door, gave the visitor the once over. She looked familiar. I noticed a large glossy red suitcase at her feet.

"Do the Blackbees live here?" she said.

"Who's asking?" I said.

"Just get your mum, will you. I'm in trouble." She reached out her right arm, used the door jamb for support.

I made a closer inspection of the visitor gracing our step; put a name to the face. It was only Strawberry Blonde Stella, wasn't it? I'd last seen her crying all over Sullivan's shoulder at Uncle Stavros' farewell do.

"Who is it?" Granny Bee said. "If it's the tallyman tell him we're not in."

"It's Stella." I said.

"Stella who? Get out the way, girl, let me through." She jockeyed past me, drew in a sharp breath, whistled as she blew out. "Well, well, Stella from Soho. Bloody hell's bells, we can all see what you've been up to, can't we?"

"Oh Granny Bee, I don't know what to do." Stella began to wail. I elbowed my way back in front.

"What's the matter with her?" I said.

"She's got a bun in the oven, that's what the matter with her. Silly cow, fancy getting herself in a mess like that."

Stella wailed louder, cradled her swollen belly with both hands. Granny Bee wrapped an arm round her shaking shoulders. I did the only thing I knew best to do in those sort of circumstances. I bellowed at the top of my voice.

"MUM!"

11

Before I had the chance to bellow again, Mum was pounding her slippered feet along the hall. Vera and Connie Doyle were breathing hard down her neck. Only a small gathering had congregated that morning to put the world right. Second Hand Sid had shanghaied Marjory Watkins off to Blackpool for the week-end. Old Ma Flowers was floored by a summer cold, which was just as well as our hallway was pretty narrow and Old Ma was pretty broad across the beam. We were used to strutting the sideways two-step with her in confined spaces, but for any male of legal consent it was an experience to be avoided at any cost. It's rumoured she takes liberties when pressed up close, and word gets round, doesn't it?

"What in the name of God is going on out here?" Mum said.

"It's Stella from Soho," I said. "The silly cow's got a bun in the oven."

Within seconds the four of them navigated Strawberry Blonde Stella along the hall.

The red suitcase was left for me to bring. It weighed a ton. I gave it a double-handed drag. By the time I made it to the kitchen the whistler was bubbling, rear-ends were parked around the table. I smelled the aroma of anticipation cooking. From the radio, Englebert Humperdinck begged to be released, he'd found a new love, wanted to trade the old one in. Sounded to me like he was a no good for nothing two-timing son of a gun.

Stella dabbed at her peepers with a soggy hankie. The other four sets did the silent communication thing that happens when nobody knows what to say. I knew then just how serious it was. Normally everyone has an opinion on everything. Normally everyone fancies themselves as a right regular Miss Proops.

The twin doors on the serving hatch opened. Dad's face made an entrance. As he summed up the situation it took on a smouldering of displeasure. I came to the swift conclusion the smouldering was for two reasons. First, odds were high he'd be hauled into women's business. Second, there was a major chance he'd miss the Sunday afternoon film.

"So where's the baby's father then?" Vera said. "I suppose whoever he is knows about the happy event."

The slamming of the serving hatch doors signalled Dad's retreat. I stood motionless beside the red suitcase, half afraid to even suck in air lest I was heard, ordered out like usual when a secret needed sharing. It was more of a challenge to earwig now I was bigger, now I couldn't disappear behind a chair, or tuck myself into a corner.

"I'm not a slapper, Vera," Stella said, "if that's what you're insinuating. Just 'cos I'm an exotic dancer don't mean I puts it about you know."

"You're a bump and grind artist, Stella, and that's nothing to be ashamed of." Vera fluffed up her bottle blond hair. I noticed half an inch of dark root on show. "In fact, I did a bit of that during the war. I was quite famous for me tassels, I can tell you."

"Expect you were, Vera Williams." Stella's voice dripped with scorn. "But I'm a proper exotic dancer. I've got the python to prove it, an' all."

I took a moment to think about the python, wondered if it was coiled up cosy in the red suitcase. Mainly though, I wondered why anyone would want to dance with a snake. Surely tripping the light fandango with a wild animal was inviting grievous bodily harm, wasn't it? I decided there was a strong chance Stella would soon be knocking on heaven's door if she chose to continue such a dangerous career. Once she was back in shape, of course. And then I wondered if Vera really did do a bit of bump and grind during the war.

"You had the figure for it back then, didn't you?" Granny Bee said. "Gone to seed now, hasn't it? Too much bloody vodka, that's your trouble, Vera."

I slid my peepers west, gave Vera a discreet up and downer. No matter how hard I tried I just couldn't imagine her in the bump and grind business, couldn't imagine her once a glamour puss, 'cos that's something of a basic requirement, isn't it. As far back as I could recall Vera had been washed up and washed out. Considering her life style it was a God given miracle she was still standing.

Now Stella, though bloated with a baby in her belly, was still an attractive package, with wide kohl lined eyes, plush lips, fine boned long limbs. I could go on, but I think you get the picture.

"Ladies, please, we're not discussing Vera's shortcomings," Mum said. "There's that many of them it would take forever and a day. So, Stella, how have you managed up 'til now? You can't have danced with a belly that big."

"I got a waitressing job, then Sullivan helped as much as he could, but times are hard, what with the club closing, and I'm scared, Mrs Bee, what am I going to do?"

A fresh wave of tears began, left clucking tongues in its backwash. Mum produced a dry hanky. Vera flashed the fags. Connie topped cups with stewed tea. Granny Bee's mind took itself off for a wander. It was obvious by the vacant glaze in her peepers. I heard the clink of spoons stirring in sugar, shovelled through the sludge of my memories, came up trumps with the one of Sullivan comforting Stella on the worst day of my life. As far as I was concerned it was clearly beyond reasonable doubt he had taken advantage of a girl in distress. And now he'd off-loaded his mistake down south for us to deal with.

"You'll stay here, Stella, that's what you'll do," Mum said. "And first thing tomorrow, best let your family know where you are, don't want any unnecessary worrying, do we? Anyway, you might be surprised once you've talked. They might help you get through this, help you make the best decision, for both you and the baby."

"Oh no, Mrs Bee, I won't tell them about the baby. They think I'm a good Catholic girl. They'll disown me if they find out the trouble I've gone and got myself into."

"Oh dear, you're in a proper bleeding pickle, aren't you?" Mum sipped her tea. Worry lines creased her brow.

"Well, it takes two to tango," Vera said. "I suppose the father's done a runner, hasn't he?"

"He doesn't know." Stella's voice was barely a whisper. I was lucky to catch the words. "He never will."

There were sharp intakes of breath. Tongues clucked again. I guessed that let Sullivan off the hook, guessed he was the good guy after all. That's the trouble with me, sometimes I'm too quick to condemn without a fair trial.

"A one night stand then." Vera rummaged in her bag for the silver hipflask. She was growing agitated, needed a vodka booster. "Should have got off at Fratton, shouldn't he."

"Or one night of passion," Connie Doyle said. "It happens."

I tipped my head east, waited for Mum's version of events, noticed her and Stella exchange a loaded look of understanding. I attempted to read the signs of the unspoken conversation. It was beyond me, but Mum understood. She heard it loud and clear.

A hush fell over the kitchen. Joe Brown took the opportunity to sing about his sea of heartbreak, his lost love and loneliness. It was a wonder there was a single dry eye in the place.

"It wasn't like that." Stella spread fingers over her belly full of baby. "We were in love."

"Women always say that," Connie said.

"Fools to ourselves, we are," Vera said.

They all sighed then, even me, even I recognised the truth in that. After all, in the name of love I was the biggest fool ever where Denny Doyle was concerned. At that point I felt great comradeship with the tea and talk brigade. We were all losers in love. My peepers trekked from face to face. I imagined they were remembering the one who got away. I still had to hook mine, hadn't so much as a nibble. Denny Doyle was as wily as the speckled pike that cruised the waters of the moat, dragging ducklings down into its murky depths by their little webbed feet. Allegedly, that is. Many had cast the catgut hoping to catch the local legend, just as many had failed, though Biffer Smith's Labrador once took a summer splash, only to howl his way up the grassy bank pretty darn quick, with a chunk of cream fur missing from his flank.

"Well, Stella, until we know what's what you'll stay here," Mum said.

I wrestled with a groan itching to escape my lips, recalled Ginger Rodney, the last out of town dosser she took pity on. He left with the milkman's money. Dad caught up with him at the ferry, buying a one way ticket to the Isle of Wight. Obviously a bit of a tussle happened 'cos Dad came home with a shiner, warned Mum to choose her dossers more carefully in future. Most now were natives on our estate who'd had a dust up with their beloveds. They usually left the next day, or were fetched by sorry looking spouses, or snotty nosed kids sent instead. And, as if I could forget, Granny Bee, the longest staying dosser in history.

"I don't want to be a nuisance, Mrs Bee," Stella said.

"You won't be." Mum's tone informed me she'd made her mind up on the matter. "Besides, where would you go? No, I've made up my mind. You'll stay here, Stella." She leaned against the chair back, noticed me with the red suitcase at my feet. I practised one of my innocent smiles. She practised one of her glares. I twitched a shoulder, redirected my peepers to the red quarry tiled floor. The tile in front of my left flip-flop had a hairline crack running diagonally. I studied it for want of something better to do. "How fortunate, here's Ruby." I heard the heavy dose of sarcasm. "Make yourself useful, if it's not too much bother. Take Stella's suitcase to the front room, please."

Four other sets of peepers twirled towards me. I took great care not to let mine latch on to any particular pair, prepared to do battle with the suitcase that weighed a ton.

"And ask your father to sort out the sofa bed," Mum said.

I manhandled the case to the front room. It used to be the lounge. Now it was the spare for dossers. When dossers weren't in residence it lay in limbo for the next invasion.

Then I backtracked to the lounge. This started out as the dining room, but as Mum pointed out, it never got used 'cos we took our meals at the kitchen table. Dad was laying low there, hidden behind the Sunday People. A fine pillar of smoke curled towards the ceiling. I smelled the scent of Sun Valley baccy. The jingle for Esso Blue played on the TV screen.

"Mum wants you to sort out the sofa bed," I said.

"I will in a jiffy," he said.

"Stella from Soho's here. The silly cow's got a bun in the oven."

"So I gather."

I perched on the arm of his chair, thought about the latest predicament, decided it was far worse than the usual. This wouldn't be just an over nighter, would it? This wasn't just a general domestic fallout. Stella had nowhere to go, no one to go to. And there was a baby to add to the equation as well. And Mum's need to rescue waifs and strays. What if Stella brings the baby here after the messy bit's done? I've seen the bliss on her face when she handles a new born. She should have been blessed with a brood of kids. If that happened we'd never get shot of them.

"So what happens now, Dad?" I said.

"I don't know, Ruby," he said.

"What if Stella has the baby here? What are we going to do with it?"

"Haven't a clue, me darlin', my crystal ball seems cloudy today." He snapped the newspaper in half, tossed it on the coffee table. "Maybe Vera can help you out with one of her superstitions."

"Maybe she can." I was growing sick of the mockery. "She was right about the crow, wasn't she? We've had a shed load of hassle since then. You did bury it deep, didn't you, Dad, like you were asked to?"

"I buried it deep enough." He vacated his favourite chair, made for the door. I tagged behind him. "And if I've told you once I've told you a million times, stop listening in on a bunch of superstitious old women. Now, help me with this damn sofa bed before we both get the cold shoulder treatment from your mother."

We staged a two-prong attack on the sofa. Dad grappled the seat skywards, I plunged my hands into its gizzards. After a short struggle we beat it into submission, though a couple of minor injuries were sustained. First a spring nipped my thumb, drew a bead of blood. Unfortunately for Dad, after a taste of the vital life force it moved in for the kill. A bracket locked its jaws around his forearm. Only after a crusade of curses did it finally admit defeat. I stored a few of the riper ones for future use. We inspected our war wounds until Mum's voice was heard drifting towards us. We arranged our faces into neutral, smiled a greeting. Stella had difficulty returning like for like. Mum had a touch of the tight lips upon hers.

"Stella will be staying for a while, Mickey," she said.

"Right-ho," Dad said.

"Sorry to be a nuisance, Mr Blackbee." Stella's words wobbled. She backhanded a rogue tear away.

"Nonsense," Dad said. I was impressed by the sound of his sincerity.

"You just need some time to think, Stella, some breathing space, to consider your options." Mum shook out a clean cotton sheet. "Don't be hasty mind; bed down here till you decide what to do."

Dad and I left them tucking in hospital corners, hightailed it to the kitchen. I had one main concern niggling away. I chose the best moment to mention it, after Dad had necked a generous measure of the cooking sherry kept in the top cupboard out of Vera's reach.

"Holy Moses." He beat his chest like Tarzan, settled himself at the table. "That's a brutal drop of cheap plonk, that is."

I sat opposite, gave him my best unblinking stare. He whistled a tune about when the saints go marching in. Eventually he said, "What? What's the look for, Ruby? I swear to God you get more like your mother every day."

"It's Stella," I said.

"What about her?"

"What if she stays, Dad, what if she never leaves?"

"Oh she'll leave. A girl like her won't put down roots in this old backwater town." He rolled a gasper, tucked it between his lips.

"How can you be so sure?" I watched him light the baccy. He indulged in a couple of puffs, blew a perfect smoke ring.

"Because I know her type, that's how."

"What type is she, Dad?"

"The restless type, me darlin', the type that lives for the bright lights."

As it happens, Dad had her nailed. Stella's stay was relatively short. Whilst she was dossing though, my earwigging went haywire. And when she did finally pack her belongings and head out, I sort of missed her, missed the hands of poker, missed the make-up lessons.

But all along she was planning to set us up, 'cos when she did a runner, she left more than her dirty washing behind, I can tell you.

12

Stella **stayed two** weeks and four days. Her total contribution to the household was a whole heap of hoo-hah. There were tears, tantrums, slamming doors. It took the heat off me though, 'cos Mum was busy smoothing the waters or engrossed in baby preparations. She hardly noticed my existence. Funnily enough, I actually missed her meddling in my affairs.

The kitchen was transformed over night into a small cottage industry. Booties and matinee coats were knitted with alarming speed. Miniature sheets and smocked nightdresses flew off the well oiled Singer. Old Ma Flowers embroidered ducks or bunnies on finished items. Granny Bee crocheted a blanket in a muddle of pastel coloured left over wool. A pram got donated from someone wanting rid of it. It was a Silver Cross with a sprung chassis, the Rolls Royce of all prams. Nobody questioned where it had come from.

"This reminds me of the war," Granny Bee said. "We all pulled together then, didn't we."

"We most certainly did," Connie said. "Let's have a sing-song."

It didn't need suggesting twice. Even now, when I revisit that short space of time, I find myself humming the red robin tune. Sometimes I sing the words about the red, red robin coming bob bob bobbing along. I still recall every line. It's inked across my heart like an old sea dog's tattoo.

When the singing dried up, Vera confirmed the make of the baby by dangling her plain gold wedding ring on a length of thread over Stella's swollen belly. I noticed how thin and warped that ring had become. It must have been a shiny new circle when she got hitched. I bet it slipped effortlessly on her finger then. I bet it was slick with dreams. Now she had to soap it past her arthritic knuckle. Now it was battered like her.

"Oh will you look at that," she said. "It's spinning anti-clockwise. You've got a filly cooking in there, Stella."

Everyone murmured sounds of excitement. Dad, paying a flying visit to the teapot, launched his eyes to the beyond. For a second I saw only the whites.

"I don't care what it is." Stella sighed.

"Of course you don't," Mum said, "as long as it's fit and healthy."

Stella sighed again, shifted on her seat. She was huge as a double-decker bus, couldn't get comfy no how, didn't seem much interested in anything either. Mum tried hard to boost her morale, encouraged her to help make the tiny garments. She shouldn't have bothered, her enthusiasm fell on cloth ears. I'd heard her tell Dad she was puzzled, the girl had no nesting instincts whatsoever, what would happen to the poor mite once it got born? Dad said the mothering would kick in as soon as she heard that first pitiful cry new babies do. Mum wasn't convinced, said something was amiss.

Anyhow, Stella decided she'd had enough of the tea and talk, lumbered back to the dossers room. I tagged after her, was bored of the baby subject, the war days, in particular Granny Bee. Playing cards was a better prospect. But after fifteen minutes Stella suddenly gathered together the deck, told me to clear off, give her some peace. She took to her bed, looked plum tuckered out. I moseyed back to the kitchen for a glass of orange squash. Getting thrashed at poker was thirsty work. Obviously it was tiring being the thrasher as well.

So I dawdled over my glass of squash in case the chit-chat had turned to something of importance. It hadn't. Then Lady Luck shone her light on me. The ladies tried to out-do each other on the gory details of childbirth. It came across as nasty, a bloody war full of pain. My lugs began flapping like bird wings in flight. I swore there and then never to get myself in that sort of predicament, which shouldn't be difficult, seeing as the opportunity to get acquainted with the pleasures of carnal knowledge was nonexistent.

"Of course having a baby now is a piece of cake," Granny Bee said. "You've got that newfangled gas and air, haven't you? Well, women had sod all in my day, sod all."

I detected a slight whistle on the letter S in her speech. That informed me her false gnashers were packed in a hanky, poked who knew where about her person. Sometimes she plucked them out of a pocket. Sometimes she left them under her pillow. Even worse, I've known her tuck them up the leg of her belly warming bloomers. It was no bed of roses living with a fruit cake, I can assure you.

"Gas and air's not all it's cracked up to be," Marjory Watkins said. "Hurts something awful either way."

I turned my sole attention on to Mrs Watkins, wondered how she knew about childbirth seeing as she was kid free. I gave her a closer inspection. Since she'd retired from the entertaining, at the insistence of Second Hand Sid, she was a different person. Gone were the short skirts, cleavage busting blouses. Her face was mainly au-natural, just a hint of pearly pink lippy, a brush of mascara. Neither did she keep the night hours company anymore. I gathered from the earwigging Sid rescued her from some beer swigging big-wig on the local Council. I heard it was love at first sight, which I found hard to believe, Sid being short and wide, and that bow-legged he couldn't stop a pig in a passage. There was no mistaking how much he adored her though, how much she adored him back. I didn't fully appreciate what a good sort he was till he helped me with my break for freedom. He might be pug ugly on the outside, but inside, he was truly beautiful.

"Oh Marjory, there's still a chance, isn't there?" Mum said.

"A very slim one, Joan." Marjory put on a smile that only touched her pearly pink lips.

"It was my decision, my one big mistake. But let's not dwell on past losses, eh."

I wondered what past losses Marjory had to dwell on, came to the conclusion it must be unrequited love, same as me. Obviously it's been about since the year dot. She and I were living proof. I wondered if Mum was too, remembered the encounter I witnessed between her and Uncle Stavros.

"Well, let's hope Stella drops this baby as quick as you did her, Joan." Vera nodded towards me. "Wouldn't even let you get to the comfort of your own bed, would she? Been a bloody nuisance ever since an' all."

Six pairs of peepers settled on me. Guzzling squash I returned their stares, strengthened it with a slight boost of the eyebrows. As I recall, the entire tea and talk brigade had gathered that particular Saturday afternoon after their weekly shop at Charlotte Street market across the waters. They made a tight little community. I was the outsider. I lowered my glass, gave them the Elvis lip. They indulged me with sympathetic smiles. Teacups were lifted, sipped from, matches were scratched, Players lit alive. Everyone was smoking Players lately. Dad had acquired a job lot from the Dockyard. He worked there as a welder, worked a few scams as well. It was something he never stopped doing, was in his blood, same as the vodka was in Vera's. I gave her a closer examination.

Picture this, a five foot two bottle blonde sparrow. A reasonable description unless you were in the know, then it became as plain as the nose on your face she was damaged beyond repair. War did that to people. Dad told me the stories. Steven Shaw next door had too. Most picked themselves up by their bootlaces, dusted themselves down. A few only managed to scramble to their knees. Vera was one of the few. Steven Shaw was another.

I grubbed around in my memory, sifted through my earwigging information. There should be tons concerning Vera, she'd been poking her beak into my business since I was a second old. I grubbed deeper. Only three facts surfaced. The first, she got married at the wrong end of a loaded shotgun. I remembered her saying she got caught out by a knee trembler down the back alley behind the Palace dancehall. She said she did it for love. She was eighteen years old.

The second was a black and white snap she once showed me. The edges were curled. It was blotchy with long ago tears, a faded red lipstick kiss. The bride was clearly her. She wore a pale coloured suit, a pill box hat sat at a jaunty angle on fair curls. The groom was Vinnie, the husband she never talked about, dark haired, handsome in his naval uniform. He met his maker in 1943. I guessed a battle on the high seas claimed his soul. But that's the problem with guessing. The odds are you guess wrong.

And finally the fact I've always known. Vera was a drunkard. The smell of vodka on her breath was familiar. Same as the smell of Trebor extra strong mints she sucked to fool us she hadn't supped Smirnoff for breakfast, or Murphy's Corner Store budget priced equivalent if money was tight. She lived by all sorts of superstitions that generally made no sense at all. If a black cat crossed her path she'd predict doom and gloom for hours on end.

New shoes should never be placed on a table, nor should umbrellas be opened indoors. And then there was the dead crow. After that incident I wondered if she really did have a point.

"Ruby Blackbee, you've not heard a word I've said, have you?" Mum's voice called a halt to my musing. She flavoured the words with a pinch of a grumble.

"I've told you before, Joan, the girl's nothing but a dolly daydream," Granny Bee said. "She'll get nowhere fast in this world if she's living in dreamland."

"My Frankie's the same." Connie Doyle sighed. I smiled at the mention of easy-going Frankie and his acoustic guitar. "Only wish Denny was the same, instead of being hell bent on breaking the hearts of the entire female population."

My smile faded. I also wished Denny would quit the heart breaking of the entire female population, would see me as more than the girl next door.

"They're young," Mum said. "Can't you remember what being young was like, all the dreams you dreamed, all the hope?"

"I remember," Old Ma Flowers said. "I dreamed of being a ballerina."

All eyes rooted themselves on Old Ma. I noted the ample bosom, the broad backside spilling over the chair seat. I visualized the image of a ballerina. Not even my wildest ideas could put the two together.

"So what stopped you?" Vera sniggered. I did likewise. "I'm sure you'd have made the perfect Sugar Plum Fairy."

"Oh shut your cakehole, Vera Williams. What do you know about anything?" Old Ma brushed Vera off with a waggle of her fat fingers. "You can't even do a half decent waltz, you can't. At least I've got rhythm. I may be a big girl, but I'm light on my feet."

"Yes, you are a lovely dancer," Marjory Watkins said. "Sid mentioned it himself at our engagement party, reckoned it was a pleasure to trip the boards with you."

Old Ma preened at the compliment, tidied her silver hair. Vera slid her a look loaded with daggers. I recalled the engagement party. It was a boozy affair, held in the back room of our local drinking establishment. Second Hand Sid coughed up the ackers for canapés and French champagne. Denny Doyle brought along a tall brunette trollop, parked her at our table, spent the rest of the evening pursuing a Cilla Black lookalike. I hoped there'd be a cat fight, but the trollop had more self-respect than I would have.

"Well, ladies, time to call it a day," Mum said. "I've a hundred and one things to do before I get to put me tootsies up."

The ladies loaded themselves with their shopping bags, left in single file like a herd of pack mules. Except Vera, of course, she'd leave when she was good and ready. And Granny Bee, 'cos she was waiting for the lift that wouldn't come to take her home to Soho.

"That Ma Flowers' got some bloody sauce, hasn't she, Joan?" Vera sniffed, emptied the dregs in her tea cup down her throat. "She can be a right old moo when the mood takes her. Fancy saying I can't dance. I did all right during the war, didn't I?"

"Different kind of dancing though, wasn't it?" Mum stacked crockery, placed them on the drainer, turned the hot water tap on.

"Bet she never jitterbugged. Well I did. Remember the Pavilion, Joan, and all those Yanks? Christ, they could shake a leg. We were flung all over the shop, weren't we?"

"That was a long time ago, Vera. Now, are you staying for a bite to eat or not?"

"Depends what you're having." She spread a sulk across her chops.

"Bread and if its," Mum said.

"Might as well then, seeing as I'm here already."

"Then butter the bread. Ruby can check on Stella. I've had a feeling about her all day, I have."

"Oh Mum, can't Vera go?" I made sure my voice had a full whine about it. "Stella's a proper misery guts lately."

Mum pretty much ignored me, apart from shooting a look my way, the one I'd learned from experience not to trifle with. To reinforce my disapproval I produced an east to west eye rotation, snorted a holier than thou snort, stamped my feet all the way to the dossers room, tapped the door, opened it a smidge, peered in. It was twilit. Stella had drawn the curtains.

"If you want a sandwich you better get yourself to the kitchen." My voice dripped with more bristle than a hedgehog's got quills.

"Help me," she said.

That plea indicated she'd wedged herself into a position she couldn't wriggle out of. I dawdled to the sofa bed, stretched out a hand to help heave her free. She grabbed it as if it were a life-line, reeled me in with the strength of Pop-Eye.

"Blimey, you're as strong as Pop-Eye." I tilted forward from the waist, noticed a glistening of sweat on her brow, a clenched jaw. A pear shaped tear trickled down the side of her nose. "What's wrong, Stella?"

"Get your Mum, please." She dragged the word *please* out so far it snapped under the strain, twanged out of tune like a broken guitar string. It didn't take a genius to work out I was in the middle of a crisis. I tried to shake her loose, stepped back as far as my arm allowed. She clung on tighter. My fingers began tingling through loss of blood flow. I didn't want them to, but my peepers swept over the length of her bloated body to the business end.

She'd hoicked her dress up. Everything was on display. You don't need the gory details to guess what was going on, do you?

"Bloody hell, Stella," I said. "What's happening to your down belows?"

She replied with a scream that near on rattled the teeth out of my head. I felt duty- bound to join in. My vocal chords jangled with the effort. Fortunately the synchronised screaming achieved the desired effect I'd hoped for. Mum came galloping into the dossers room, Vera in hot pursuit.

"Oh my giddy aunt," Mum said. "Somebody get the midwife, Mrs Stubbs, number forty-four. Quick."

"No time, it's coming now," Vera said. "You go, Joan, hurry. I'll do what I can here."

Mum barged between Dad and Granny Bee loitering in the doorway. I wished it were me fetching Mrs Stubbs the midwife. The tingling had spread to my wrist, my fingertips were tinged blue. I worried the hem of my blouse with my spare hand. From the radio in the kitchen I heard the faint voice of Gene Pitney telling us he was gonna be strong. I decided I should be too.

"Do you know what you're doing, Vera?" I said.

She finished spreading a clean towel across the sofa bed, gave me a leisurely study. I noted her peepers were perfectly focused. I was more accustomed to seeing them blurry with booze and bad memories.

"Well, you're still here, aren't you?" Her voice sounded cool. "Besides, I did a bit of nursing during the war."

"Thought you were a bump and grind artist," I said.

"I was. I did a lot of things, some I'd rather not recall. Now belt up, Ruby, a miracle's about to happen."

For the rest of my days I'll never forget the gentle way Vera eased the purple dappled scrap into the world, its first lusty cry. When I think back on that afternoon it takes the black out of my darkest mood and colours it gold.

"It's a boy," Vera said.

"Are you sure?" I stretched my neck to check. "You reckoned it was a girl."

"Of course I'm sure. Oh he's just so gorgeous."

"He looks like a skinned rabbit," I said.

Mrs Stubbs bustled in, took over. I noted her tartan slippers, a navy headscarf holding a bunch of pink rollers in place. Stella gave up the grip on my hand. I massaged it back to life, watched Vera move away, watched Dad fold her in his arms. She slumped against him for a minute then wrenched herself free, left the room. I guessed the new birth had taken its toll on her, prayed she wasn't on the edge of a relapse, prayed Stella's days of dossing were on the countdown. But my prayers fell on deaf ears. God wasn't listening.

13

While **Mrs Stubbs** the midwife finished her job, the rest of us had a cup of rosy. Except for Vera of course, who'd done a Houdini, who Mum said was heading for a cropper. And if that wasn't enough worry to be going on with, Stella couldn't be persuaded no how to part with a name for her newborn son.

We sat for a while incommunicado, with only the rattle of cups on saucers, the tick of the big old kitchen clock breaking the silence. I was famished, decided to fix myself a sandwich, slapped ham between bread, a scrape of Branstons. I kept my lugholes finely tuned, hoped for some enlightening conversation to start. I wasn't kept hoping for long.

"So when's the tramp leaving?" Granny Bee said.

"What tramp?" Mum said.

"That tramp from Soho, Joan, whatshername."

"Do you mean Stella?"

"Yes, that's her, pretty girl but looser than a whore's ..."

"Don't be nasty, Duchess," Dad swiftly interrupted.

I felt my lips lift a smirk. Monty, the marmalade cat, sloped across the kitchen tiles to cadge a ham taster, practised his leg weaving until I caved into his demands, dropped a slither of fat. We chewed in unison.

"Facts are facts," Granny Bee said. "You weren't there, Mickey. Well, I was. Hell's bells, you'd need a shoe horn to prise them apart, they were that chummy."

"Prise who apart?" Dad said.

"Stella and whatshisname, and he's up and disappeared, hasn't he? For God's sake, the whole world's gone stark raving mad."

I stopped chewing, wondered if she was referring to the elusive Black Jack Baloo, wondered if he'd done the dirty with Stella seeing as Sullivan hadn't. Dad must have wondered the same.

"Do you mean Jack?" he said. "Do you know where he is, Duchess?"

I waited for Granny Bee's answer. Whilst waiting I made a plan. Once I learned the whereabouts of the prime suspect connected to Uncle Stavros's untimely demise, I'd hotfoot along to the phone box on the corner of Nickle Street, inform the cops, who in turn would arrest the son of a B with the fondness for Russian Roulette. I hoped the boys in blue found it in themselves the need to rough him up a bit. Or even better, rough him up a lot. Maybe a couple of broken bones. After all, it was near over six months since the worse day of my life.

The earwigging had offered little new information, only stories of my Uncle's shenanigans that brought wistful smiles to faces, or tear sodden eyes, or short silences while memories were re-wound. By all accounts it was just my good self still festering over Jack getting away with murder.

"How the hell would I know where Jack is?" Granny Bee slurped her tea, stared into space. I swivelled my peepers in their sockets. "Did he make it home from the war? Plenty didn't, you know."

"Of course he made it home." It was clear Dad was struggling for composure. I glanced at Mum. Her lips were pressed tight together. "Think hard, Duchess. When did you last see Jack?"

I took another bite of ham and pickle. Granny Bee and thinking could possibly be a long, painful process. It was. I'd finished the sandwich, plus a wedge of Victoria sponge.

"Trafalgar Square," she said. "May, nineteen-forty-five."

"Trafalgar Square?" Dad raised one dark eyebrow, held it high for a moment, let it drop to rejoin the other.

"That's right, Mickey, Trafalgar Square, nineteen-forty-five, VE Day. We did the Lambeth Walk clean round Nelson, didn't we? Surely you remember that."

Dad made a frustrated sound, hoisted himself to his feet, strode a few paces, stared out the kitchen window. He gripped the edge of the Butler sink that tight his knuckles almost burst through skin. I snorted, made sure it was on the heavy side of scorn.

"Jack and I were still in France mopping up blood and guts, Duchess. Please accept my sincere apologies for not making it back for the celebrations, but someone had to do it."

"Mickey, don't say any more. It's not her fault." Mum tutted, drew her chair closer to Granny Bee, patted her hand.

"Well, for Christ's sake." Dad forced out a lungful of air, scratched his head with both sets of fingers. His face was pinched white, his eyes dark, broody like a bloodthirsty buccaneers. He returned to the table. I stayed where I was, out of the firing line. "I just want to know where Jack is. How hard can it be to remember something that happened not that long ago?"

Granny Bee blinked twice in slow motion. Her bottom lip quivered. The double layered chin rippled. Monty made a hasty exit. I heard him scale the stairs to safety. My heart stepped it up a beat. The baby with no name began a weak mewing from the dossers room.

"He's giving me that look, Joan. His own mother no less. I've seen that look before. It scares me, Joanie, tell him to stop it."

"Stop it, Mickey," Mum said. "You're scaring your mother."

"I'm sorry, Duchess, I just want to know where Jack is, it's important."

The baby continued to cry, revved it up a decibel. I noticed my parents trade a fleeting glance with one another, noticed Dad was still brooding. I couldn't quite figure out Mum's expression. Naturally, if I'd known beforehand what Granny Bee had to say next, I would have recognised it as despair.

"Anyway," she said, "Jack will be with the Greek boy, the one who was sweet on Joan. Then you came back, Mickey, and she chose you, and broke that poor Greek boy's heart."

The three of us gasped in perfect harmony. My jaw dropped south. I recalled the conversation with Rita Swan about the Greek sailor, about the Blackbee boys not being full blood brothers. I recalled the scene I'd witnessed through the serving hatch doors that last Christmas. I wasn't stupid. I saw for myself those buried desires bubbling under the surface of virtue. I wondered if Dad did too. It didn't bide well for Mum's reputation, did it? Especially as everyone knew Uncle Stavros had been a skirt chaser extraordinaire.

The baby sounded distressed. I tried to block out the sound of his wailing, tuned in to Buddy Holly singing about a whole lot of women shedding tears for a brown eyed handsome man. It reminded me of my uncle. His eyes were the darkest brown I'd ever seen, that dark they sometimes seemed black. I wondered if Mum also remembered. I slid my peepers left, settled them on her. As usual she recovered her wits about her first.

"I've always been Mickey's girl, Duchess." She made for the door leading into the hall. "Now what's going on with that baby? I'll just pop and check everything's all right."

"And I'm going to the pub." Dad packed his smoking paraphernalia into his trousers pocket, followed behind her. "I feel the urge for a Saturday night skin full."

"And when you get back, Mickey, we need to talk." Mum turned, stopped him in his tracks with the flat of her hand against his chest. I stopped putting two and two together, kept my lugholes fully cocked. The need to talk was a serious matter.

"Talk, Joan?" I watched disappointment crawl across his face. "Talk about what?"

"I'd rather not say at the minute, not with Big Ears listening in." She nodded towards me, straightened his shirt collar, smoothed the backs of her fingers down his left cheek. "Just don't have too many whiskeys this evening, that's all I ask."

They continued on their way. I heard the front door click open, click shut. I heard muffled words from the dossers room. As I was at a loose end, I gave Granny Bee a piping hot glare.

"What are you glaring at?" she said.

"You," I said. For good measure I gave her a bare toothed growl. "You're a trouble maker, you are. Fancy saying Mum broke the Greek boy's heart."

"'Cos that's exactly what she did. What do you know about it anyway? You weren't there. Well, I was. She kissed him like she meant it, right in front of Nelson. You'll find out about that sort of kiss when you're older."

"I've kissed a boy already, I know all about that sort of kiss." I repeated the bare toothed growl, supported it with a curl of the top lip.

"No, girl, you're still a kid, you don't know nothing yet. Wait til you get the real deal." She heaved herself standing, grimaced as she straightened her spine, took a couple of stiff legged steps. "Then God help you, 'cos you'll need all the help you can get, I can guarantee that. So leave me alone. I'm going to my room."

But she got no further. The exit was blocked by Mum and the wailing baby. I put on my disgusted face. She was wearing a worried one. The baby's was furious.

"We've got a problem," she said, "with Stella. A big problem."

It took a lot of willpower to keep those well used words *I told you so* to myself. Right from the start, when the door bell chimed those opening bars of God Save The Queen, it was obvious she'd brought a problem along with her. I didn't see why it was ours though. But I couldn't think straight, since the baby with no name continued to bawl his head off. For someone less than a day old, he had a fine set of lungs. Maybe I should offer to go buy him a dummy. They sold them at Murphy's Corner Store, hanging on a card, in a choice of pink or powder blue.

"How come it's our problem?" I raised my voice a few decibels. "He's Stella's baby."

"Yes, he is, but it's pretty obvious, isn't it, Ruby?" Mum rocked him up and down, backwards and forwards. His puny legs escaped from the shawl, kicked the air. His fists were balled. "Stella has rejected her own son. Now, put the whistler on, sweet pea, let's get a bottle made. This boy is hungry."

I lit the gas. Yellow fire licked up the sides of the whistler. I adjusted the flame. It changed to the colour of a sky in high summer. Granny Bee settled back down on the chair, held her arms out, took the baby. She peeled his shawl off like she did a Jaffa orange. Mum measured Cow and Gate into a bottle, joined Etta James in a song about how her lonely days were over, about how her heart was wrapped in clover. I had the uneasy feeling she was singing it for the baby with no name.

"But what's it got to do with us, Mum?" I said.

"For the moment it's got everything to do with us," Mum said. "We can't let the poor little mite starve, Ruby, we can't sit idle and let that happen, can we?"

Put like that I had nothing to build an argument on, so I looked through the open kitchen door instead. Although it was late evening, the air was still warm. Outside I smelled the perfume of the sweet lavender planted in a wooden tub. A weak breeze flapped the curtain of multi-coloured plastic tape, its purpose to hinder pesky flies from making an aerial advance indoors. It didn't always do the trick. If one made it through, Mum hounded her quarry to death with the spray, pumping lethal mist like Al Capone pumping bullets from a self-loading sub-machine gun. Dad preferred the rolled up newspaper method.

The whistler began to hum. I returned my attention to the grim situation I'd found myself in, through no fault of my own for a change. Mum poured water on milk, gave it a shake. Granny Bee shushed and cooed. The baby continued to bawl. I decided to make myself scarce, before I got roped in to help.

"Where are you going, Ruby?" Mum said.

"I'm going somewhere quiet." I made sure my tone was on the long suffering side, added one of those heavy sighs that tugs the shoulders up to your lugholes, watched her attempt to lift the baby out of Granny Bee's arms. They tussled over him for a second. Mum won, made herself comfy on the chair. After a brief grumble, Granny said she was retiring to her room, she'd had enough of the present company for one day.

"It'll be quiet once he gets this bottle inside him." She tucked a clean nappy under his chin, slipped the teat between his lips. He took it greedily.

A dribble of milk slid down his chin. He sucked, rested, sucked, rested. When he stopped to rest, air bubbles raced to the surface. I noticed dark and plentiful hair, cotton thin veins beneath flawless skin. A bootee worked loose, fell to the floor. His toenails were as tiny as the fragments of busted shells rolled into shore by the tide. My peepers roved up again, met with his. They were the colour of soot. Something stirred behind my ribs, somewhere in the heart region. It made my chest ache. I wondered if it was tenderness. Before it could take a hold I pushed the wondering away, could do without getting emotional over a baby that wasn't staying.

"He's not likely to cry all night, is he, Mum?" I said.

"Of course he won't cry all night, Ruby. Look at him. He's exhausted already, poor little lamb. He's had a hard time, you know, it's not easy being born."

I looked at him, thought he better get acquainted with the hard times pretty damn quick, 'cos there were plenty of them on the horizon with Stella as his mother. He yawned.

Even though I wasn't tired, I followed suit. Hours rolled by. Babies are time wasters. I heard the sound of distant whistling. Mum heard it too.

"That's your father on his way home." She glanced at the kitchen clock on the Welsh dresser inherited from an Aunt Mimi I'd never met. Dad had sanded it back to the bare wood, glossed it delphinium blue. A set of plates, hand painted with crimson roses, were displayed on the grooved shelves, brass bells picked up from day trips to places like Brighton or Bognor cluttered the wide one above the double cupboard. Every week those bells were rubbed with Brasso, buffed up bright with an old rag. Sometimes I helped. It was a tedious job. I had to be bored senseless to bother. "Oh good grief, he's whistling that bloody song. I bet you any money you like he'll be singing it in a minute."

She was right. A few seconds later the whistling stopped, slurred words started. The pipes the pipes were calling him, from glen to glen and down the mountain side. The volume indicated they were also calling him up the side path to the back door.

"I told him not to get whiskeyfied." Mum placed the sleeping baby in the pram, tucked blankets around him, spooned Nescafe into a mug. "Scoot your backside to bed, Ruby, I don't want any witnesses to see the damage I'm about to inflict on another human being."

Fortunately, I had a plan, so I went quietly. I reached the half landing where the stairs turned, sat down on the third step from the top. It was a safe place to be, invisible from the kitchen, but still in earwigging range. If necessary I could tilt forward a fraction, grab a view of the action between the banisters. The smell of instant coffee wafted up from the kitchen.

"So you're home, Michael George Blackbee." I couldn't resist a chuckle. If Mum addressed you by your full name, you'd probably feel the blast from one of her famous tongue lashings next. "And you're the worse for wear by the looks of you, an' all. You're nothing but an old fool, aren't you, and that's the truth."

"So I'm home. Have you missed me, darlin'? Have you missed this old fool?"

The sound of a chair scraping tiles made me praise the Lord for such good fortune. He was whiskeyfied enough to need to sit. The kitchen table was in my line of vision. I wondered if I should take a gamble, tilt forward before I missed anything. But before I could decide a voice hissed in my left lughole. My heart kissed the soles of my feet. I thought, of all the gin joints in all the towns, she walks into mine.

"Are you spying, you nosy little beggar?" Granny Bee said.

"Shush." I held a finger to my lips.

"Is it the French Resistance?" She squatted beside me.

"No, it's more important than that."

"Is it Operation Overlord then?"

"No, Granny, it's even more important than Operation Overlord, so you must be as quiet as you can, else we'll get caught and shot at dawn, and it'll be all your doing."

We sat side by side on the third step from the top. My peepers did a westward slide towards Granny Bee. Her fine hair was flattened beneath a flesh coloured net, her face shiny with the Nivea she used before bed. She needn't have bothered; it hadn't kept the wrinkles at bay. A bubblegum pink winceyette nightie brushed her brown slipper boots with the front zips. I prayed I wouldn't end up in the same state as her.

"Will we be long," she said, "only I've got no bloomers on."

"Shush," I said, peeped through the banisters, saw Dad take a mug from Mum's hand.

"I wanted to talk to you about something serious, Mickey," Mum said.

"Go ahead then, Joan, I'm all ears, but first, let me just say, whatever it is, I'm truly sorry I'm a little worse for wear. We were only wetting the baby's head, but there was six of us, and one round led to another. It's hard to say no, isn't it?"

"For you it is, Mickey, but it's the baby I want to talk about."

"There's nothing wrong with him, is there?" I heard a slur of concern in Dad's voice.

"No, there's nothing wrong with him. Oh God, Mickey, I know who his father is." I heard the hitch of a tear, a sharp intake of breath. "He's your brother's child, Mickey. He's Stavros' boy."

My mouth hung slack in disbelief. I noticed Dad's did too, noticed he sobered in record time, without assistance of the black coffee either. I turned to Granny Bee.

"Holy bloody mackerel," I said.

"Holy bloody mackerel indeed," she said. "I didn't even know he had a brother. Must have been from another lifetime or something."

Once again the Greek sailor came to mind, then Uncle Stavros, then the baby with no name. I thought about Granny Bee, about her memory lapses, her troubles with the here and now. Although our dislike was mutual, I still felt sorry for her, felt sorry that she couldn't remember her own son.

"Yes, Granny," I said, "it must have been from another lifetime."

14

I laid beneath the summer weight blankets. As usual the bedroom door hung ajar. The landing light was on. Through a chink in the curtains I saw a yellow half moon, a cluster of silver stars, a navy blue sky. I wondered if Uncle Stavros had made it through those pearly gates, wondered if he rued the day he played Russian Roulette, wondered if he ached for the son he never got the chance to meet. But mostly I wondered about the latest piece of earwigging.

Who else knew the baby with no name was my Uncle's child? Did Big Shirley? Or Sullivan? After all, they helped Stella out when she was down on her uppers. Come morning though, I was certain Granny Bee wouldn't remember sitting with me on the third stair from the top, listening to a conversation that didn't concern us. But as sure as God made little green apples, I would remember.

The murmur of muffled words continued in the kitchen. It was highly unlikely I'd catch a wink of sleep before dawn. The restless hours would all be for nothing, an' all. When we met again for Dad's famous Sunday fry up, my parents lips would be shut tight. No matter how much hint dropping I dropped, they'd waltz around it as graceful as Fred Astaire and Ginger. I blame the war. Keeping secrets was a habit then, and habits are hard to break.

I obviously dozed 'cos the smell of Vera's vodka breath roused me from my slumbers. I opened a peeper. There she was in the flesh. So she hadn't come a cropper yet. Mum would be relieved.

"How long are you going to loaf about in bed?" she said. "Breakfast is ready. Get your lazy bones off this mattress."

The aroma of Dad's famous full fry up proved she was telling the truth. Then I recalled the earwigging last night. Knowing what I knew put the dampers on my appetite. I just couldn't face the crispy bacon, sausage, fried eggs sunny side up.

"Go away, Vera. I'm not hungry." I gave her a one-eyed glare. She leaned in, gave me a look loaded with suspicion. Stale vodka fumes hit my snitch with the strength of a storm force ten. She placed a clammy palm against my brow. I pulled the summer weight blankets higher. She pulled them lower.

"Well, ain't that hard cheese," she said. "I've been sent to fetch you, so get your miserable self moving before I makes you."

I flicked both peepers cautiously across her ugly mug. The last time she made that threat I was five. It was the summer. Antonio's pink ice-cream van kerb crawled the estate. He was Eyetallyano, permanently tanned, dark hair shining like spit and polished boots. So the story goes, he started life in England as a POW, banged up in a camp on the edge of the Hard with a view of terraced houses to the east. Westward, at low tide, he enjoyed the sight of boats marooned on the mudflats. After the war he never returned home, 'cos he'd fallen for Elsie, a local girl from the row of terraces, had courted her through the camp fence, passed her love letters, promised eternal devotion.

Anyway, that day Vera met me from school. We stopped at Murphy's Corner Store, spent the last of her cash on sweets for me, put a bottle of Smirnoff on tick for herself. And then I heard the tinny jingle, the one that coaxed kids from the safety of their homes like the Pied Piper. And I knew I wouldn't be having an ice-cream as well, 'cos God forbid you should spoil a child. So I did what I was best at. Back then tantrums came naturally to me.

Now the thing with Vera is she never gives you the luxury of an option. If only she'd told me to stop or else, I'd have stopped, 'cos or else was a fate you didn't want to find out about. Instead, just as I was getting into the throes of a full blown screaming abdab she grabbed two fistfuls of grey pinafore, hauled me along the street like a side of beef. But soon I'd be sixteen, was bigger, braver. She was older, vandalised by vodka. Nowadays she'd find it difficult to make me do anything I didn't want to do, wouldn't she?

"Well, Vera." I put a sneer on my face. "I'm not a kid anymore. You can't make me do anything I don't want to do."

She made me. There was wrestling involved. I couldn't get a grip on her, she was as slippery as a greased snake. We grappled our way out to the landing until Mum interrupted, shouted from the kitchen, "What the devil is all that commotion about? Sounds like a herd of bloody elephants up there."

We broke apart. Vera straightened her skirt, patted her bottle bleached hair. I retreated, gave her an eyeball laced with venom, wondered if it was worth going for another round.

"What commotion?" Vera said.

"Don't give me what commotion, Vera Williams. Jesus Christ, I thought you were coming through the ruddy ceiling. Get down here, the pair of you, breakfast is getting cold."

I shrugged into my dressing-gown, slipped feet into slippers, made for the stairs. Close behind I heard Vera chuckle, felt her hot breath singe my left lughole.

"Don't think this is the end of it, Vera," I said.

"Don't be such a bad loser, Ruby," she said.

I stopped mid-flight. We squared up to one another. I pushed my face into hers.

"I'm not, you were lucky. Next time I'll be ready for you."

"You were lucky I went easy on you." She pushed her face closer. I noticed she'd gone heavy on the pressed powder that morning, noticed her lipstick was a darker red than usual.

"Now get moving, before you feel the force of a Boston Stranglehold."

I got moving, braved a snort over my right shoulder, but truth be told, I half believed she might be capable of putting the Boston Stranglehold on me. The breakfast table seemed the safest place to be. We sat opposite each other, kept our peepers apart, tackled our fry ups.

"So, you going to tell me what all that commotion was about, or shall I bring out the thumbscrews?" Mum said.

"We were skylarking around, Joan, that's all," Vera said.

I gave her a glare. Dad lowered the paper, glared at everyone. I could see from the set of his lips he was unreceptive to small talk. I guessed he was still dealing with last night's bombshell. The cause of that bombshell was peacefully kipping in his pram. From the radio Jim Reeves asked us if he was that easy to forget. Well, there was fat chance of forgetting the baby with no name, not with Blackbee blood running through his veins.

"Skylarking around?" Mum said. "Aren't you too old for that sort of thing?"

"You're never too old for a skylark, Joan," Vera said.

"I hope you didn't hurt my sweet pea." Mum looked me up and down. I gave the breakfast my full concentration. "Best watch out that competitive streak of yours don't get the better of you, Vera, what with you being the champion mud wrestler of '44."

"Hang on a minute." I stopped the nattering with my fork poised mid-air. "Is that the God's honest; Vera's a champion mud wrestler?"

"Oh yes," Mum said. "Didn't you know?"

I laid my fork carefully on the plate, folded arms across my chest. Dad's peepers briefly skimmed over the top of the paper. I recognised a certain amount of glee in them.

"No, actually, I didn't." I put a layer of sarcasm into those few words, pushed my plate away, couldn't eat another bite. "Nobody tells me anything, do they?"

Nobody felt inclined to comment. I wasn't surprised. The baby with no name began to grizzle. Three women rose, circled the pram like a Cherokee war party. Stella was holed up in the dossers room. Dad stayed behind the paper. As I had a prior engagement that morning I cleared off to get ready. It was our estate's football match final. Frankie and Duffy were in the team. The church youth club organised it. Competition was fierce. So was Father O'Hara. For a man of the cloth he had no fear of wading into the thick of a fisticuff on the pitch. He was highly respected by his flock of faithfuls , mainly for his generosity with the holy communion wine. The non-believers respected him for his lack of judgement. And me, a small time serial sinner, it was for his never-ending forgiveness when one sin followed hot on the tail of another.

I foxtrotted it to the Doyle's, rapped the back door with my knuckles, entered without an invite. Mr Doyle was at the yellow Formica table. He'd recently switched jobs, was now a night watchman. Dad reckoned the work suited him; he got paid for sleeping his shift away on a narrow put-me-up.

Grace was weaving beads into her long hair. I was glad I'd made the effort, had drawn a daisy on my cheek, worn a tie-dyed T-shirt. The summer of love may not have fully embraced the estate, but we sure as hell were doing our best with such limited resources at hand. It wasn't easy; there were too many leftovers from the war stuck in their ways, who weren't interested in smelling the roses.

"Crikey, Ruby, you're on time for a change," Grace said, "must be in trouble."

"Boyfriend trouble," Mr Doyle said.

"I don't have a boyfriend." I dropped onto a chair, heard the sour grapes in my voice.

"Well you will have, and he'll be no good for you, that he will." He stared into his coffee. I wondered if he was having a vision, if he could see who the boyfriend was, if it would happen any time soon.

"Can you see who he is, Mr Doyle?" I was thinking of Denny. If any boy was no good it was bound to be him. The thought wasn't unpleasant, even though, without a doubt, he'd break my heart, lie and cheat, take everything a girl had to give, then cut himself loose without so much as an adios. To tangle with Denny Doyle was a foolhardy risk. And I was more than willing to be the risk taker.

"Oh Ruby, what's to become of you?" Mr Doyle looked me dead in the eye.

"How do you mean, Mr Doyle?" I straightened up. A part of my future was ready to be revealed. I felt a little afraid, same as I did when I once spent a tanner on a palm reading with Gypsy Rose at the Easter Fair. She told me not to trust a fair-haired stranger who offered adventures in a foreign land.

"I see upsets, Ruby, that's what I see in store for you."

"Well, you're right there." I snorted. "I've got those upsets you see already. He was born yesterday, the baby with no name. Nobody wants him, not even his mother."

"Somebody wants him." Mr Doyle stood, made to leave. I watched him go. An uneasy feeling set up residence in the pit of my belly. I already knew who that somebody was, Mum. She would mourn his leaving as if he were her own. I might mourn his leaving as well now I'd discovered who half of him belonged to. It might be like losing my Uncle all over again.

"Come on, Ruby, let's go," Grace said.

We left via the back door, linked arms, strolled towards the rec. The morning was a scorcher already. Heat rose off the grey paving slabs. Underfoot, the tar on the roads felt soft.

"Grace," I said, "what your dad was saying earlier, about the boy who won't be any good for me."

"What about it?" she said.

"Do you think he meant Denny? 'Cos he's the only boy round here who's no good, isn't he?"

"I don't know, Ruby, he just senses things." She gave my arm a shake. "Besides, you're bound to meet another boy that's no good, aren't you?"

The burnt grass was already dotted with bodies of lounging spectators by the time we arrived. The rival teams were having a last minute kick around. I noticed Frankie warming up. He noticed me, smiled. I smiled back, ambled over to join the gang of scallywags I hung out with, spread myself next to the skate bait called Rosemary Collins.

"Where were you yesterday evening?" The smell of her musk perfume drifted across the foot or so of no man's land between us. "A Yankee ship's in. It was a riot last night."

"I'm not interested in sailors," I said.

"Of course you're not." She gave a sly grin. "Still holding out for Doyle, aren't you."

I pushed my Lennon shades in place, unwrapped a Wrigley's, carefully considered the words for a lie of denial. I shouldn't have bothered, 'cos I knew Rosemary had a little gem of know-how for me tucked up her sleeve, suspected it was going to hurt like a kick in the teeth. It did.

"Don't look now, Ruby." Her voice dripped with delight. "But lover boy's over there with his latest squeeze."

Naturally I couldn't stop my peepers from following her line of vision. Lover boy was indeed canoodling with his latest squeeze. I gave her the once over, didn't recall ever seeing her before. Maybe she was new to the area. I gave her another look. She was a cut above the average, a long limbed green eyed brunette, bronzed by the sun. She shifted, shoved Denny away, flicked her hair off her face. I noticed the tide mark of a tan as she adjusted her short denim shorts. Denny noticed too, ran a finger along the line. She swatted him off.

"Poor cow." I shrugged, leaned back on my elbows, made a plan. I'd sit it out until half time, then leave, plead a headache, or sunstroke perhaps. And that's how I happened to spot in the distance Stella from Soho, on my solitary walk home nursing a freshly broken heart. And what's more, she was on the loose, hadn't even taken her baby out for a push in the pram. I supposed Mum was left holding the fort. Stella was the most selfish person I'd ever met, and that's saying something, 'cos it took a lot to beat Granny Bee at that game.

As usual I found Mum sat in the kitchen hemming a skirt. It was the size of a tent, guessed it was for Old Ma Flowers. A packet of Rich Tea lay open on the table. Frankie Vaughn sang about an old piano playing hot behind the green door. From the dossers room I heard the baby fussing.

"Baby's crying." I reached for a biscuit, nibbled around the edge the way I liked to do.

"Your Granny's just gone to tell Stella it's his feed time."

"Stella's not here." I parked my posterior on a chair.

"What do you mean, Stella's not here?" Mum stopped hemming.

"I saw her about fifteen minutes ago, walking along the main road."

"Where was she going?"

"I don't know." I hitched a shoulder, helped myself to another biscuit.

"I know where she's going." Granny Bee turned up with the baby cradled in her arms, joined us at the table.

"Where's that?" I said.

"Away from here, that's where."

"Don't be ridiculous, Duchess, she hasn't got any money." Mum's eyes travelled to the top of the dresser, settled on the Queen's Coronation cup. I watched her get up, walk to the dresser, fetch it down. "It's bloody empty. She's stolen the milkman's money. You wait til I get my hands on her. I'll give her what for, the little..." and she used the B word, the one she once called the flighty strumpet from number ten.

I sighed from the soles of my flip-flops. The milkman had been fleeced a second time. She should have listened to Dad after the Ginger Rodney incident. Out of town dossers weren't as trustworthy as the locals.

"That girl will come to a sticky end before long," Granny Bee said. "But at least she left a note."

A sheet of paper was laid on the table. Mum scanned the words, closed her eyes. Her face turned white as bleached bone. I wondered about the baby with no name. What would happen to him?

"What's going to happen to the baby?" I said.

"She wants us to keep him," Granny Bee said. "That's what she put in the note, and a whole lot more."

My peepers roamed east, fixed themselves on the note. Mum slipped it from view, folded it twice, placed it in her apron pocket, said, "You can't just give a baby away in this day and age, Duchess."

And I agreed. Apart from the fact that giving babies away was highly illegal, there was no room for him in the house, no room for him in our lives either. My parents couldn't expect me to tolerate yet another unwelcome hanger-on, not without some strong resistance at the very least. The Seekers backed me up, said the carnival was well and truly over. It was time to part company. I decided to air my feelings about the matter, made the mistake of taking too long to choose the right words. Granny Bee beat me to it.

"Stella's not really giving him away though, is she?" she said. "And in any case, blood's thicker than water, Joan. That's got to count for something, doesn't it?"

I sighed. I'd been so certain Granny Bee wouldn't remember sitting with me on the third stair from the top ear-wigging on a conversation not meant for our lugholes.

15

*V*odka Vera breezed in at four-fifteen, peeled off her cardigan, exchanged a meaningful look with Mum. She worked six days a week at the local watering hole, had been there as far back as I could recall. The job was right up her street, the regulars subsidised her liquor requirements, the wage met the rent, fed the gas and electricity meters, kept her topped up with Smirnoff. It didn't stretch to much else. Her cupboards were as bare as Mother Hubbard's, but it hardly mattered; she generally sat at our kitchen table for meals. Although a lot had happened in the hours she'd been gone, she found us as she left us that morning.

"What's going on here then?" She checked on the sleeping baby, parked her scrawny rump on a chair, slid a hard-nosed look my way. "She been riding roughshod over you all again, 'cos if that's the case, I'll give her one of me famous Chinese burns."

I slid Vera the best self-righteous glare I could muster at such short notice, muscled it out with a upper lip twitch, felt my fist itching to lead the way forward, weighed up the pros and cons of a rematch with the former mud wrestling champion. In my favour I had the enthusiasm of youth, was fitter, faster, but untrained in the art of grappling. She had the experience of age, had beaten me once, but was hampered by years of chain-smoking and fire water. Duane Eddy made his guitar sing about a rebel rouser. I considered it a fitting piece of music to take me into battle. Unfortunately, Mum intervened.

"It's Stella." She poured tea, stirred in sugar, passed it across to Vera. "She's done a runner."

"What do you mean, done a runner?" Vera's thinly plucked eyebrows vanished beneath bleached curls. "She's just had a baby."

"And she's left him here," Granny Bee said, "for us to keep."

I screwed my peepers onto Granny Bee with the full force of utter contempt, added a sniff on the weighty side of total disrespect. She reimbursed me with an unblinking stare. Her sour expression told me nothing, but I wasn't as dumb as she thought I was. Behind those sly old eyes the wheels were still turning. Trouble was, I couldn't be sure which year they were turning in.

"Christ knows what Mickey will say when he gets home," Mum said.

Eddie Cochran began a story about the summertime blues. Granny Bee took to the floor, started to dance a loose version of the Hokey-Cokey. She threw both arms in, both arms out, in out in out, she threw them all about. I knew what was coming next so threw my peepers east, concentrated on Eddie singing, decided any minute soon I too was gonna raise a fuss, was gonna raise a holler.

"So what's the plan, Joan?" Vera said.

Eddie faded away. Acker Bilk took over. I fine tuned my earwigging radar, watched Granny Bee waltz to the table. Monty the marmalade cat leaped upon her lap. The small bell attached to his collar jingled. He arched, settled down, purred loud as a knuckle swollen hand smoothed along his body. He anchored amber coloured eyes onto mine. We'd reached a settlement, the cat and I. He didn't attack if I didn't attempt to stroke him. It suited him better than it suited me, but I wasn't about to beg for his friendship.

"There isn't a plan, Vera." Mum clattered cups and saucers together, dumped them in the sink, opened the oven door. The smell of roast beef escaped.

"What?" Granny Bee sat straighter, dislodged the cat. He stretched a back leg. She clucked him back up. "No plan, Joan? Where would we be if Churchill had said that, eh?"

"Up the flaming creek I expect," Mum said.

"Yes, that's exactly where we'd be. I hope Manny Wise's eldest son didn't sacrifice his soul in vain, Joan, just because you didn't make a plan. All he's got left is Rudi by his second wife, and he's only interested in making the devils music."

"What's the devils music, Granny Bee?" I said.

"Rock and roll, that's what the devils music is. That young buck Presley started it. Wears his guitar like a weapon, he does, slings his pelvis all over the shop." She folded her arms, lifted her bosoms. "I know what he's suggesting. I didn't come in on the last banana boat, you know. That sort of thing should only happen under the cover of darkness."

Mum and Vera chuckled. I chuckled as well, although I thought it probably best if my initiation into the smooching with intent took place under the cover of darkness too. As it happens, when I finally gave a boy the green light, the occasion was lit by moonshine, the air sweet with the scent of clover. I believed it was the real thing. Turned out his idea of love wasn't the same as mine. Doctored punch had a lot to answer for.

"Well, the baby needs a home, Joan," Vera said, "and it's clear as day you've bonded with him as if he were your own."

"It's not that simple," Mum said.

"But it could be. You said she left a letter, and there's a blood tie, isn't there?"

"Mickey will never agree, and it'll cost money, Vera, money we haven't got."

"Oh Joanie, let's at least think about making a plan."

"Better think quickly then. Mickey will be home soon."

I earwigged on the making of a plan, doubted it was likely to work on someone as smart as my Dad. For a start it was riddled with the truth. If I were them, I'd drop a whole heap of the hysterics on his shoulders, layer it thick with the boo-hoos. If that didn't sway the odds in my favour, I'd accuse him of abandoning his brother's child, accuse him of being a heartless son of a you know what. For a change, Granny Bee had nothing to contribute.

I heard Dad whistling his way round to the back door, recognised the tune, Billie Holliday asking why fools fall in love. I asked myself the same question. As usual, no answers were available.

"Ladies." Dad greeted us like he always did, took his place at the head of the table.

I tilted my peepers slightly west, watched Mum and Vera prowl across the tiles, balancing dishes of roast spuds, veg, a platter of thinly carved beef, Yorkshire puds, a jug of steaming Bisto. They flanked him. He had no escape. My heart lurched. I straightened up the already straight cutlery.

"Mickey, I have something to tell you." Mum set the dishes on the table. We began to help ourselves. "And I'd rather get it done without interruption, if you don't mind."

"Sounds serious." Dad laughed an uneasy laugh, waggled his curled fingers in a give me more gesture. "Come on, Joan, it can't be that bad. Let's have it."

She let him have it. As he ate he listened, learned all about Stella doing a runner, abandoning the baby, leaving a letter. Occasionally he raised an eyebrow. I pushed my dinner around. Vera picked at hers. Only Granny Bee tucked in. Just lately she'd developed a fondness for tomato ketchup, dolloped it on everything. Her plate bore a resemblance to a mafia shoot-out.

"Of course what she suggests is impossible, isn't it, Mickey?" Mum said, but I heard a different question being asked. I heard her asking to keep the baby with no name, heard her asking for a miracle. I thought only divine intervention could pull that trick off.

Dad rose, left the table, checked the pram. The baby was still in residence. He returned, kept his peepers steady on Mum's. She held out Stella's note. He took it, scanned the words, glued his eyelids shut. When he eventually prised them apart, his eyes were as black as jet.

My heart beat took up the quickstep.

"Jesus bloody Christ," he said.

"She must have been desperate, Mickey." Mum leaned towards Granny Bee, wiped ketchup off her mouth. "No mother just walks out on her baby."

"If you ask me, you're best shot of that baby." Vera sniffed, rummaged in her handbag, brought out a pack of Woodbines. "Get on to Social in the morning, Joan, put them in the picture. Perhaps then things will get back to normal round here."

And I agreed. It would be for the best in the long run. That baby was no age, yet already he was the keeper of memories. And not all of them were good ones.

"Nobody's asking you, Vera." Dad slid his half eaten dinner to the side. "Maybe we should think a bit more about Stella's letter. Our old bigwig Shuffles in Soho still owes me a favour or two. I'll take a trip up there next weekend, see where we stand." He fetched a tin of Sun Valley from his pocket, a packet of blue Rizla, rolled a choker. He flipped the lid on his Ronson. The smell of lighter fluid drifted my way. I heard the grind as he spun the tiny wheel saw his left eye squint as he fired up. "And now, ladies, I shall mow the lawn, and I don't want to be disturbed."

And I knew he knew there wasn't a hope in hell I wouldn't be disturbing him as soon as I'd cleared the table, helped wash up, tidied away. As I did what was expected of me I ear- wigged. It proved worth my while.

"The Lyons had sugar cubes, you know," Granny Bee said. "That's where I went for my secret rendezvous'. Of course I was a lot younger then. And afterwards we'd take a stroll and canoodle underneath the arches."

"Good job those arches don't tell tales then, ain't it, Mrs Bee?" Vera said.

"Well somebody did. Bloody hells bells, I thought he was going to kill me."

My lugholes went on full alert. I turned my attention west towards my grandmother.

"Who was going to kill you, Granny Bee?" I said.

"Whatshisname, that's who," she said.

"Who's whatshisname? The man you had a secret rendezvous with?"

"Oh no, he didn't rough me up. He was such a gentle soul. I wish I knew what happened to him though. I hope he didn't get fed to the fishes."

"Don't upset yourself, Duchess." Mum smoothed a hand across hers. "There's no point raking up the past."

"But I still worry about it, Joan. That bloody river's full of unfortunates wearing nothing but a pair of concrete boots."

I forced myself to stay calm, waited for more. Nothing else followed. I wondered if the gentle soul was the Greek sailor, wondered if it was my granddad who roughed Granny Bee up. Minutes passed. It seemed another secret was sinking faster than a poor unfortunate wearing nothing but a pair of concrete boots. So I rushed the tidying away, made a sharp exit left through the back door into the garden. It was early evening, still warm. The sun floated low in a pale pink sky. Yellow honeysuckle hugged the back fence, spread itself over the shed roof. The scent was as sweet as icing-sugar. Mum's roses were head heavy. Their thorny stems bent under the weight. Bees were having a serious boogie-woogie. A Red Admiral took a breather on the neatly clipped lavender. Dad pushed the mower up the lawn, down again. The blades spun, cuttings sprayed into the grass box. I fell into step beside him. In silence we walked up and down twice more. He broke first. Sometimes he found me as irritating as a splinter stuck under your skin.

"Now what, Ruby?" he said.

"It's about that baby." I decided to get straight to the point. "He's barely two days old and he's messed everything up already."

"You can't blame the baby, darlin', he didn't ask to be born."

"But the longer he stays the harder it'll be for Mum when Social takes him away."

"So what would you have me do, Ruby? Not try at all and break your mother's heart? Some rotten husband I'd be then wouldn't I, if I didn't at least try?"

"But her heart will be broken anyway, won't it, Dad, in the long run?"

"Maybe it will, but I won't be the one who breaks it." He draped an arm around my shoulders, pulled me in for a squeeze. I buried my face into his shirt. It smelled of Daz and faint sweat. I listened to his heart beating strong and even. He planted a kiss on the top of my head. "Hey, how about me and you having a dance this fine evening. Have I taught you the polka yet?"

I shook my head against his chest.

"Then it's high time you learnt. We'll dance to our song. I'll lead, you follow. It's dead simple, just a one two hop. Even you and your two left feet can manage that. "

We faced each other. He placed the flat of his hand against the small of my back. It felt warm through my cotton blouse. I placed my palm on his shoulder. Our free fingers linked together. He began to sing about me, his Dixie darlin'. We stubbed toes a few times 'til I got the hang of it. I smiled up at him. He smiled down at me. We twirled around the half mown lawn at full speed, beheading daisies and disturbing the bees.

And then I had a thought. What if the poor unfortunate wearing concrete boots was the Greek sailor? What if it was Granddad George who roughed Granny Bee up? And what if Black Jack was twiddling his thumbs somewhere in Soho, the very place Dad was planning to go? There and then I decided he needed protection on the visit with Shuffles the bigwig. And, obviously, I was just the right person for the job.

16

I knew there would be strong opposition about my decision to escort Dad to Soho. Therefore, the only option left open was to become a stowaway. It would take precision timing, but I could do it if Lady Luck made the effort to smile down on me.

From the earwigging I learned Dad would leave on Friday after dinner, stay overnight at The Bee Hive, seek out Mr Shuffles the next morning, then travel home. It gave me plenty of hours to build my defence, 'cos as sure as the devil wears horns, it would be the hottest water I'd get myself into yet.

So, the one chance to sneak into the back of the car would be when Dad said au revoir to Mum. She'd go through that routine of asking a dozen questions before letting him go. I could almost hear the conversation due to take place. If she was on form, it might take him five minutes or more to break away. I reckoned on needing three minutes tops to scoot down the side alley, slither into the car, curl up on the floor behind the driver's seat under the assortment of blankets kept for emergencies, such as being stranded in the wilderness. No doubt it would be tight, but it was all in the preparation. I had five days to practise sprinting, to try and shave seconds off my fastest time. As it happens I only had a day and a half before Mum made an appearance.

"Why are you stampeding up and down this alley like a rampaging elephant?" she said.

I stopped short. The stitch was pricking my right side. I turned to face her, a lie already forming on my lips.

"I'm not," I said.

"What are you doing then? And don't lie. I've told you before, nobody likes a liar or a thief."

I took a moment, thought her remark about liars and thieves a bit rich considering she was happy to be a regular receiver of black market goods. So I felt on safe ground to tell another lie to cover the first.

"Actually, I'm sprinting." I sighed as loud as I could. "I'm taking up sport, getting fit."

"Sport? You?" She snorted, crossed her arms, narrowed her eyes. I heard the sarcasm loud and clear. "It takes all your energy to get yourself off the mattress every morning."

"Well it's true." I put on my indignant voice. "Why doesn't anyone ever believe anything I say?"

"I'm sure I can't think of a single reason why." She threw an eye roll to be envious of. When they settled back down in their sockets, they sought me out like a pair of heat-seeking missiles. "Perhaps it's something to do with your track record." She wagged a finger in my direction. "But I'm warning you, Ruby Blackbee, I know you're up to something and it better not be trouble."

I thought it prudent to keep quiet. Past experience had taught me that on some occasions it's best to say nothing at all, especially if you were up to no good. I waited until she'd padded away indoors, then scuffed my feet past the border of blue lobelia incarcerated behind the chain link fence, to lean against Dad's old car parked kerbside on the road. As usual it was spit shiny, chrome bumpers sparkling like new, windows smear free. And as I leaned I watched Grace and Duffy stroll along the pavement towards me, arms glued around one another, hips bumping. A growl attached itself to my vocal chords. I wasn't in the mood for her pity, and that's what I'd get if she thought I was all on my lonesome.

"What are you doing, Ruby?" She stopped, smiled.

"Wasting time," I said.

"Come and waste time with Duffy and me then, listen to some records."

I wasted some more time thinking about it, took pleasure at the way Duffy's mouth tightened with annoyance. Recently we seemed to get on each other's nerves more than usual. And it was pretty obvious why. I was the third person in a relationship meant for two. The gooseberry. One of us should bail out. If I was that great a best friend, it ought to be me. We both knew it. Only Grace didn't.

"I don't think so, Grace." I fixed a bored expression on my face. "As Dylan says, times are a changing. Seems like you and me are too, seems like we're not travelling on the same road anymore."

"What do you mean by that?" Grace said. "We're best friends, Ruby, what's going on?"

"Nothing's going on. We're just after different things, aren't we? You want to get hitched and have babies, I want adventures. Won't get any of them hanging around this dead hole, will I? I'll be good as gone as soon as I can,

London, probably, where it's all hip and happening."

"Oh." She sounded hurt. "I didn't know that's how you felt."

"Well now you do." I gave Duffy a look. Before he came on the scene Grace and I were as close as Siamese twins. Not even a crowbar could have separated us. I pushed myself off the car. "Anyway, must go, places to be, people to see." I strolled down the street, cursing under my breath with every step I took. Truth was I had no place to be, nobody to see.

I reached the end of Nickle Street, halted, wondered whether to turn right, meet up with the gang at the rec, or left, into town, browse the shops, maybe listen to a few 45's at HMV. I hadn't been holed up in the booth listening to the latest chart releases for quite some time, decided it may put me in a better frame of mind, set off at a brisk walk, hadn't gone a dozen paces before I became aware of a motorbike cruising alongside, revs dropping, engine barely ticking over. I tilted my head east. Denny Doyle's grin greeted my scowl. I kept walking, belly fluttering, pulse picking up speed.

"Where you going?" he said.

I put the brakes on. So did he. My peepers roamed over him, noted the tight black T-shirt, oil-streaked Levi's, battered Chelsea boots. A warm breeze lifted the hair of his brow. I saw my reflection in his metallic tinted shades.

"As far away from here as possible," I said.

He smiled, hooked a finger, slid the shades down the bridge of his nose, checked me out from top to toe. I had the itch to treat him to a knuckle sandwich, shoved fists into the pockets of my faded jeans.

"Well I'm taking this beauty for a blow out." He lovingly patted the petrol tank. "How about you coming with me."

My heart missed a beat, then broke into a gallop. I made a show of considering the offer, didn't want to appear too keen.

"You got a licence for this heap of shit?" I said.

"Nope," he said.

"Thought not. Where you planning to go?"

"The beach road." As he spoke my peepers watched his mouth. His upper lip was thin, the lower one plump. The two front teeth were slightly crossed. Dark stubble coloured his chin, spread to his cheeks, met with narrow sideburns. "So how about it then, unless you're scared or something."

I heard the challenge in his voice; saw the mockery in his baby blues. As I'm not the sort of girl who backs off from a dare, I curled a sneer his way.

"Scared of what?" I made sure I put plenty of scorn into the words.

"Getting arrested? Or being alone with me, maybe?"

"Don't flatter yourself, Denny Doyle." I managed a pretty good laugh.

"Climb aboard then, Ruby." He pushed the shades into place. "Let's see what this heap of shit can do."

I climbed aboard. My thighs settled behind his. My belly pressed against his back. I slipped arms around his waist, breathed in the smell of him. He throttled the bike. We rolled forward. I held on to him tighter, pressed my chin into his right shoulder blade. We reached the beach road. I felt the power of the machine beneath me as he flicked through the gears.

We were flying. I let out a whoop, and another. The wind tore the sound from my throat, threw it to heaven. Too soon I noticed we were slowing, turning into Lifeboat Lane, where the yellow flowering gorses ran amok, where lovers go to canoodle.

Denny shut down the engine. I swung off the bike; found my legs were shaking, staggered a couple of steps. I filled my lungs, tasted the salt carried on the air. My eardrums vibrated with the screech of gulls calling. Closing my peepers, I raised my face to the warmth of the sun, re-lived the dream of being up close to my heart's desire.

"You all right, Ruby?"

I abandoned the re-living of the dream, focused once more on the there and then. The bike was resting on its stand. Denny sat side-saddle, ankles crossed. Over his shoulder I saw the green-grey sea. Lazy white tipped waves lapped at the shingle beach.

"Yeah," I said. "I'm all right."

"Well, we clocked ninety, give her a tweak and I reckon she'll do a ton easy." He reached out, wrapped fingers round mine.

"We could have been killed," I said.

"No chance." He tugged me forward. We were inches apart. I remember praying to God not to let me faint. "Only the good die young. You know what, Ruby? If you were older, you'd be the type of girl I'd go for."

"I'm nearly sixteen," I said.

"And I've got a few more years on me."

"Who's counting numbers, Doyle?" He turned my hand over, ran a thumb across the palm. My insides threw a double back flip. I waited patiently for the next move. It was agony, what with patience being a virtue I was unfamiliar with.

"I'm going to kiss you," he said.

"Okay," I said.

"You know how it goes, don't you, Ruby?"

"Yes, I've been kissed loads before."

I recalled the few kisses I'd previously exchanged with potential boyfriends. Comfortable kisses, mouths resting softly together. I had the inkling a kiss from Denny Doyle would be far from comfortable, and far from soft. I wondered if it would take me to heaven and back, like Maureen from the Co-op reckoned.

"Are you ready?" Denny said.

"I've been ready for ages," I said.

He cupped my face with both hands. My eye-lids fluttered, closed. His lips rubbed slowly over mine, once, twice. He snaked a hand through my hair. The other wandered to caress my rib cage. I drew in a shocked breath, twined arms around his neck, felt fire in the pit of my belly. The kiss deepened, grew a little on the rough side. Our mouths opened in mutual agreement. Our tongues danced their own exquisite dance. As we separated, his sharp teeth nipped at my lower lip. I do believe I paid a brief visit to the ever after.

"Still got a lot to learn haven't you, girl?" he said.

"You could teach me," I said.

"No, I really couldn't, Ruby."

"So one measly kiss is all I'm getting?" Anger niggled at the initial feeling of disappointment. I damped it down.

"Jesus, imagine if your dad ever found out I'd even just kissed you. He'd hang, draw and quarter me. That ain't a risk I'm willing to take for no-one. Get on the bike, Ruby, time to make tracks."

That anger, the family trait Mum said I inherited from Dad, began to get the better of me. I walked away before I got arrested for assault.

"I'd rather walk than get on that bike with you, Denny Doyle." I walked faster. "You can stuff it where the sun don't shine."

"Awww, come on, Ruby, don't be so stupid. It's a three mile hike. Just get on the bloody bike."

I started to run, heard Denny shout something, but didn't catch the words. I kept running til my legs refused to run any further, sat on a convenient garden wall. He didn't come after me. I knew he wouldn't. I looked around. No chain link fencing marked the boundaries in that neck of the woods. Every house had wrought iron gates, bay windows, tarmac drives leading to their garages, front doors protected by porches. The whole area smelled of luxury. As I took a breather I wondered how long it would take to make it to Nickle Street. I must have been in desperate need 'cos my guardian angel sent a helping hand. A gruff voice interrupted my wondering.

"What the hell are you doing all the way out here, Ruby Blackbee?"

It was Second Hand Sid, Marjory Watkins' new beau. Some folks said he was a saint the way he turned up and whisked her off the road to ruin. Some said not many would take on a woman like her.

"Walking home," I said.

"Want a lift?" he said.

"Wouldn't mind." I scrambled off the wall, opened the car door, recalled Mum's warning about hitch-hiking or accepting lifts from strangers. "You're not one of those mass murderers, are you, Mr Sid?"

"Do I look like a bleeding mass murderer?" he said.

I considered the question, gave him the once over, decided he looked more like James Cagney, the Yankee Doodle Dandy, only his accent wasn't right, nor right for round here too.

"Guess not. I don't suppose you're a kidnapper either, are you?"

"No, I'm not a kidnapper either, but rest assured, Ruby, if I was, I'd soon return you pretty damn quick. Now do you want a lift or not? It makes no odds to me."

I got in the front, slouched on the passenger seat. The radio was playing. Don and Phil Everly were lamenting how love wounds and mars any heart not tough, or strong enough, to take a lot of pain. The song was made for me. Second Hand Sid pressed the accelerator, cocked his head to one side.

"Hear that?" he said.

"Hear what?" I said.

"Exactly." He smiled. I noticed he had the most beautiful smile I'd ever yet seen. "She's sweet as a nut. Soon shift this baby off the forecourt."

He drove with one hand on the wheel, the other on the gearstick. I stared out the window, wondered how I could have thought a measly kiss was the start of something, especially when I knew Denny Doyle was no good and never would be. It was obvious all I'd had was a little dalliance with the devil. I wish I could tell you I didn't dare dally a second time, but I did, I dallied with someone's affections, and I shouldn't have. And it all backfired. And I'll tell you something else; my guardian angel only sent Second Hand Sid and his wheels to the rescue again, didn't she?

17

riday happened exactly as I expected. After dinner Dad disappeared for a spruce up, Mum knocked together a stack of cold beef sandwiches, wrapped them in greaseproof. As an afterthought she cut a generous chunk of rich fruit cake, the sort that's so heavy it lies in the belly like a lump of lead. I smelled the cinnamon she uses, saw the red cherries.

"I wonder if he'll want a flask of tea," she said.

"Christ Almighty, Joan." Vera took the thermos from Mum, placed it back in the cupboard. "It's not a bloody picnic he's going on."

"Well I know that much, Vera."

"Then stop fussing. Come and have a puff and a nip of brandy. Calm yourself down."

They sat at the table, lit chokers. Mum took a long drag in, blew smoke out on a sigh.

Vera rummaged through her handbag, produced a miniature bottle of brandy, splashed a measure into their empty teacups, said, "Purely for medicinal purposes, this."

They sipped and puffed in silence for a while. I pretended to be engrossed in my Jackie, had reached the Cathy and Claire problem page, had an inkling I might earwig something worth earwigging pretty soon. Granny Bee cradled the baby with no name. He was full of milk and sound-o. Sometimes I watched him sleeping. Sometimes I thought I was more than a tad fond of him. But most times I reminded myself he wasn't really ours. He'd come into the world on a whim, and we were paying the price for it.

"I hate Mickey going to Soho alone," Mum said.

"Not 'cos of Rita, I hope," Vera said.

"She's always wanted him, hasn't she? Even before I did. Nothing's changed."

My lugholes took flight. I re-read the problem page, didn't want the rustle of paper to publicly announce my presence.

"Oh Joan, you've been married twenty odd years. If Rita had stood any kind of chance with Mickey don't you think it would have happened by now?" Vera treated herself to another nip of medicine straight from the bottle.

"And she knows too much. Mickey's not the forgiving sort, Vera."

"There's nothing to forgive, is there, Joan?"

I heard the curiosity in Vera's voice, chanced a shufty through my fringe, saw them latched together in an eye lock. Mum broke first, turned away, but not before a shadow of something very similar to guilt brought a flush to her face. I rifled through the debris of my memories, remembered what I'd seen through the serving hatch New Years Eve. I rifled deeper, remembered Granny Bee letting slip about Mum kissing Uncle Stavros like she meant it. I wondered how far that kiss had really taken them.

"Of course there's nothing to forgive." Mum stacked crockery, walked briskly to the sink. "But you know what Rita's like. She'd fancy up the innocent into something sleazy."

"What on earth are you talking about, Joan?" Vera joined Mum to share washing the crocks. As usual she was the dryer. "What's Rita got to do with anything?"

"Oh shut up, Vera."

Dad appeared in the kitchen carrying his tatty army rucksack. He smelled of Camay soap, Colgate toothpaste, a fresh pressed shirt.

"Nice to hear you ladies getting along so well," he said.

Mum turned, dried wet hands on her apron.

"Oh Mickey, what on earth are you using that moth-eaten monstrosity for? What's the matter with the brown leather holdall I bought from Charlotte Street market?"

"This moth-eaten monstrosity has seen me through thick and thin, Joan. It even saved my life once. Have I told you how it came to have this bullet hole here?" He surveyed a frayed hole with a critical eye.

"Many times, Mickey, many times." She brushed fluff off his sleeve. "Now don't start with the stories else you'll never get going. I don't want you driving late at night. I'll only worry."

"I haven't heard that story, Dad." I moseyed over, poked my finger in the bullet hole with frayed edges. "Did a German sniper nearly get the better of you?"

"Your mother says there's no time for stories right this minute, me darlin'." He gave me a squeeze, dropped a kiss upon my head, made a move towards the front door. Mum followed him. Vera continued drying up. Granny

Bee kept cradling the baby. From the radio Fats Domino told us how he'd found his thrill on Blueberry Hill. I slipped out the tradesman's entrance, lay low in the side alley. I knew the procedure. Dad would pack his bag on the passenger seat. Mum would run through a list of previously prepared questions. There'd be at least one essential item she'd insist he couldn't live without. To keep her happy he'd return to the house for that one essential. That's when I'd stow myself behind the driver's seat beneath an assortment of blankets. I smiled as I heard her begin.

"Did you put fresh underwear in that bag, Mickey?" she said.

"No I didn't, Joan. Who the hell cares if I wear my pants two days running anyway?"

"I do, Mickey, I care. What about pyjamas? Take the blue striped ones I got you for emergencies, in case of fire or something."

"If there's a fire I'll put my trousers on." Dad's voice struggled to keep calm. "I have all I need, a toothbrush and wash kit. Old soldiers travel light, Joan."

"You've room for a clean shirt at least, nothing worse than a man in a grubby shirt."

"All right, I'll take a poxy shirt, woman, and that's it. I mean it, Joan."

"I don't know why you have to be so awkward, Mickey. It's not as if one shirt weighs a ton, is it?"

I listened to their footsteps backtracking, Dad grumbling, Mum still trying her best to add to his load. I waited for the front door to click then scooted down the alley as if the devil himself was giving chase, skirted the rear chrome bumper, slithered into the foot well behind the driver's seat, huddled under the assortment of blankets, wrapped arms around my knees. It seemed ages before Dad returned, opened the car door. I heard a stream of ripe words, the thud of something heavy hit the seat, knew it was the brown leather holdall, knew that along with the poxy clean shirt there'd be fresh underwear, blue striped pyjamas for emergencies, maybe a jumper in case it turned chilly. He shouted cheerio, blasted the horn as we set off on the journey to Soho. My heart galloped faster than the winning racehorse at the Grand National. It sounded that loud I was surprised my travelling companion didn't hear it knocking against my ribs. The radio crackled to life. Some old cowboy called Hank was falling in love, wanted the door closed to temptation. Apparently the object of his desire belonged to another.

I risked a wriggle, wondered if stowing away was such a bright idea, wondered how long it'd take to get where we were going. I could feel the onset of cramp in my left leg.

Maybe I should try to kip. My eyelids dropped as The Bachelors begged Diane to wait for them. Dad joined in with the begging. I begged for sleep, doubted it would come easy. I was too uncomfy, too hot under the assortment of blankets, as itchy as a moggy hosting a flea party. Songs came and went. The eight o'clock news reporter delivered the latest updates on the elusive Che Guevara, the Vietnam war. The weather forecaster told us what we already knew, the summer of '67 was a poor one. I heard the radio click off.

"You might as well get yourself up front, Ruby," Dad said. "Don't want you throwing up a perfectly good dinner in my car."

I sucked in a breath. My lungs held it captive, my head became dizzy. For seconds I hallucinated on lack of air, eventually grabbed a gasp.

"Well come on." Dad's words were snappy. "I know you're there, squished up on the floor."

I attempted to unfurl. The cramp fought me tooth and nail. I took a breather, tried again. It was agony. I crawled through the gap between the front seats, settled down, rubbed blood back into my legs.

"Does Mum know about this?" I gingerly flexed my limbs.

"She knows," Dad said.

"How cross is she?"

"I think it's safe to say she's bleeding furious, Ruby. In fact, she said if you ever try to pull a stunt like this again you'll be out of the world faster than you arrived."

I wallowed in a little self-pitying silence. Bleeding furious was more than I had anticipated. Naturally I'd roughly calculated the depth of trouble I'd be in, roughly calculated the number of days solitary confinement I'd be sentenced to, but bleeding furious meant a lifetime of suffering. It meant my failings as a good daughter would be picked over by the tea and talk brigade, like vultures cleaning up a carcass. It meant Vera would hurt me with one of her famous Chinese burns.

"You better explain yourself, young lady," Dad said, "before I take you home and feed you to the lions."

"I didn't want you to go to Soho on your lonesome, Dad." My voice clearly sounded pathetic. I put a bit of bristle into it. "Mum says she hates you going there alone and Granny Bee says there are bodies in the river wearing nothing bar a pair of concrete boots."

"Soho's my patch." He gave me a sideways glance, twisted his kisser into a snarl. "I was born there, ran the streets, played the game. There's nothing I don't know, nothing I can't take care of."

"But you're not in the game any more, are you, Dad?" I tipped my chin east, noticed a cold glint darken his grey eyes. I'd seen that look once before, on the day of Uncle Stavros' farewell party. I didn't much care for it then either. "Maybe the rules have changed an' all. Every game has its rules, doesn't it, Dad?"

"The game never changes, Ruby. And rules are made to be broken. Now, what shall I do about you?"

I sat straighter, sensed a reprieve within reach. Chances were, if I returned tomorrow along with the good or bad update about the baby with no name, my stowaway stunt might go on the back burner, be dealt with at a later date. Of course the later the better would suit me best, 'cos given time Mum usually managed to cool down from boiling point.

"Take me with you, Dad, please, I promise not to be a nuisance," I said.

"You already are," he said.

"Then I promise I won't cause any more trouble."

"How much more trouble can you cause, Ruby? Strikes me you're already in it way past your lugholes."

"Then I promise not to ever pull a stunt like this again, cross my heart and hope to die."

I drew a cross over my heart, meant every word I said. Unfortunately I didn't know then what the future would bring, didn't know then just how many promises I'd break in my life time.

"Oh, well, that makes all the difference, doesn't it, you crossing your heart?"

I detected a note of sarcasm, chose to ignore it. Instead I said, "So how did you know I was in the car, Dad?"

"Your mother told me. Nothing gets past her. Thought you'd have worked that out by now."

"Is she always going to know everything?"

"Yep, that's pretty much how it is, me darlin'."

"Bloody hell." I felt a sulk coming on, swivelled my head westwards, stared out at the passing fields of corn as yellow as the sun. I wound the window wide open, sniffed in countryside, the smell of earth, the scent of flowers and leaves, heard the twittering of birds.

"So you're taking me home to feed me to the lions then, Dad?"

"Well, it's no less than you deserve, isn't it, my girl?" He fired a roll-up, took two quick puffs. "But we've come this far, not much point wasting petrol."

"You won't regret it, Dad." He gave me a narrow eyed look. I tested out a smile on him. He didn't care to share one back. "I promise to be that quiet, Dad, you won't even know I'm there."

"Don't make promises you can't keep, Ruby." He stubbed the butt in the small ashtray pulled from the dashboard. "You and quiet ain't the marrying kind. And I'll tell you something else. The rate you're going, you'll be toasting your tootsies in hell with only old hairy toes himself for company."

I declined to comment, was on my way to Soho, where Big Shirley probably had information on the Black Jack business, where Uncle Stavros had left his ghost. I remembered Mr Doyle once said places soak up the essence of lives that had lived there, wondered if my uncle's spirit was strong enough to send me a sign. But until I was safely through The Bee Hive's doors, I decided it was in my best interest to butter Dad up, 'cos considering the flak we were both due from Mum on our return, I wouldn't put it past him to personally deliver me to old hairy toes himself in that fiery pit called hell.

"See Mum bullied you into bringing the brown leather holdall." I gave another smile. His face didn't even bother to try. "Bet it's got more than a poxy clean shirt in it."

"You're right. It's full of your stuff. You've got spares of everything imaginable and more. The weight of it will drag your arms clean out of their sockets when you lug it upstairs. Hope you don't expect any help from me. I'm not feeling in a very generous mood this evening."

"Okay, I won't. Anyway, I'm tougher than I look." I suspected the rest of the journey would be spent in silence. As long spells of silence made me twitchy I turned the radio on. "Can you by any chance get a pirate station on this contraption, Dad?"

"Leave it as it is, Ruby. I'm not listening to that Jagger boy telling me he can't get no satisfaction."

So I listened to Del Shannon telling me all about searching in the rain for his runaway, wondering what went wrong with their love, a love that was so strong. And I wondered if love was really worth all that pain.

18

I strong-armed my attention back to our destination. There couldn't be many more miles left to travel. The countryside had given way to quaint villages, then suburbia took over with its sprawling avenues of semi-detached housing. Finally we hit the city. Dusk was beginning to breathe life into people who preferred the dark hours. Colourful neon signs lit the fronts of clubs, pubs, casinos, tempting fun seekers through their open doors. The dim insides swallowed up the takers, spat out the beat of music. I heard jazz, pop, rock-n-roll. Steve Marriott told me he picked his girl up on a Friday night.

The smell of roasting chestnuts wafted through the car window. I saw men in suits, ladies in cocktail dresses. Long haired boys in loud shirts and blue jeans paced the streets like birds of paradise. Kohl eyed girls, short skirts and belly grazing tops, pranced along like a flock of stick-legged flamingos. I wondered if Strawberry Blonde Stella had returned to Soho, wondered if she ever thought about her baby, ever thought about taking him back. I kept my peepers on the look-out for her.

The car paused at a junction. Outside Rocky's Casino a hurdy-gurdy man worked the handle of a barrel organ. A tinny version of *Pack Up Your Troubles* played on repeat. Tethered by a length of chain, a tiny chattering monkey sat upon his master's shoulder. They wore matching crimson coats trimmed with gold. It suited the monkey better, the man too worn down with years to carry off the glitz.

After a couple more right turns Dad pulled up outside The Bee Hive. Windows and doors were still boarded, although graffiti artists had made use of the once blank canvases, had spray-canned ban the bomb slogans, painted pictures, some large, others small and beautifully detailed. Erica had left a phone number offering a Swedish massage, satisfaction guaranteed. Perhaps Jagger should have given her a buzz, seeing as he was complaining he couldn't get none.

We sat for a while, Dad and me, just looking at the club where my family had worked the days, dreamed their nights away. I imagined he was replaying the past. I was too, only I didn't have as much to replay as him. At least he had good times to dwell on along with the sad. My short acquaintance with the place was nothing but upset, lurking with secrets I couldn't get to the bottom of.

"What a waste," Dad said.

"You could open it again, couldn't you?" I said.

"I'm not talking about the club, Ruby. Come on; let's get indoors before we get done for loitering."

We vacated the car. I heaved the brown leather holdall onto the kerb, dragged it forward. Dad slipped the army rucksack over his left shoulder, pulled a tangle of keys from his trousers pocket. Before he'd even selected the key he needed, the green door swung inwards. A slim built man glared at us. I gave him the once-over, he gave me a snarl. Same as on the first visit my jaw dropped south when he spoke.

"Mickey, me old cocker, still got the squirt hanging off your shirt-tails then?"

It was Big Shirley. I didn't recognise anything about her except the Scouser accent. Gone were the frocks and wigs, the shaped eyebrows, the carefully applied slap. I gave her another once over. Only the periwinkle coloured mules gave a clue to her inclination.

"Jesus, Shirley, I thought the place had been taken over by a squatter." Dad laughed, scratched his head. "I've kind of got used to seeing you in frocks."

"Not much call for frocks nowadays, is there? Since you closed the club singing for me supper's a bit of a rarity. No-one wants poor old washed-up me doing the Bassey."

Her tone was overloaded with accusation. I thought she had every right to feel hard done by. Dad hadn't considered the consequences of his actions when those club doors closed, had he? He hadn't considered the exotic dancers like Stella, or the go-go girls, or the barmaids, or the singers, or the fledgling bands who honed their skills round the drinking establishments. A lot of livelihoods had bit the dust 'cos of him. Or maybe 'cos of Black Jack. After all, he started that chain of events, him and his fondness for Russian roulette.

"Budge over, Shirley, and let us in," Dad said.

"I'm a bleeding bingo caller now." She took a step back. "Can you imagine what that's done to me, a professional artiste, calling out numbers on ping-pong balls?"

"Don't start giving me the sob story." Dad inched through the door. I followed, hauling the brown leather holdall with both hands. As far as I could recall nothing had changed. The ebony sideboard with mother of pearl still occupied space against the wall. The heavy duty door leading in to the bar was still shut. "You're living here rent-free, aren't you? I could easily sell the place, or burn it, cash in on the insurance."

"Yeah, and I'm grateful, Mickey, but it's for your benefit as well, isn't it?"

Big Shirley took the lead upstairs. I left the holdall in the hall, would need a fair bit of time to manoeuvre it up two flights before reaching the attic bedroom, didn't care to miss out earwigging on a promising piece of important information. As I brought up the rear I wondered what benefit Dad got from her living rent-free at the club.

We reached the kitchen with its lily-white cupboards and long run of beech worktop. I snuck through the brick arch into the dining-room, they walked to the engine end. I heard water running, the strike of a match, a pop as fire met gas. Tea was in the making. I sat on a straight-backed chair at the chunky table, my lugholes on full alert. With any luck they'd forget about me. I was blessed to find my luck was in.

"Any news, Shirley?" Dad said.

"Nope, not a sausage, though tongues are wagging. We'll have a legend on our hands soon, like bloody Robin Hood."

"Let them wag if they've nowt better to do. Christ, I wish I knew where that bugger Jack was holed up."

"Well, one thing's certain, Mickey. He was pretty cut up about what happened."

"Then why run, eh, before the cops could talk to him?"

I almost gave a disgusted snort. Since when had Dad been as thick as two short planks? It was obvious why Black Jack had absconded. His game of Russian roulette had backfired, at Uncle Stavros' misfortune. If he showed his portrait anywhere near Soho the cops would slap a murder tag on his head. I was as sure as heaven's happy the boys in blue would eventually brush Jack's collar, unless I got to him first. Then they'd more than likely be brushing mine. It was just a question of time before he or me did a stretch.

"I don't know why he did a runner, Mickey. I only know he was in a real bad way, wouldn't listen to reason. You won't find him, no-one will, not unless he wants to be found. It's easy to disappear in a place like this."

At that point the whistler screamed for attention. The smell of boiling water scalding tea leaves drifted my way. I heard the rattle of cups meeting saucers. The earwigging was over.

"Where's the squirt gone then?" Big Shirley said.

"Christ, I forgot about her," Dad said. "Bet she's been flapping her damn lugs. Bloody liability she is."

I moulded a half smile across my kisser, rose from the straight backed chair, poked my head round the bare brick arch. Dad was leaning against the sink. Big Shirley finished loading the pink tea-tray, became aware of me. Our eyes engaged in a mind reading match. She lobbed a message of suspicion. I smashed a volley of swear words back.

"Better fetch the holdall, Ruby," Dad said. "It's getting late."

I felt the weight of tension in the air, as thick as the souper that every so often brings the ferry boats to a standstill. I left without starting a verbal disturbance, not even a whine escaped my kisser, skipped a quickstep down the maroon stair carpet, hopscotched across the black and white hall tiles. The holdall lay where I'd dumped it in anticipation of the ear- wigging. I flexed my arms to ready them for battle, gripped the handle, lifted. That's as far as it got, 'cos it was then I noticed the door to the bar was ajar.

Puzzled, I lowered the holdall, glanced around the hall, up to the first floor landing. I would have bet my last dollar the door had been shut tight. The idea of taking a nosey began to run through my mind. Any consequences I might encounter if caught didn't even make it to the starting line. I knew they wouldn't, I'm like that, like a cat too inquisitive for its own safety. I only hoped I had one of my nine lives left.

My fingertips made contact with wood, gently pushed. I could hear my heart ratatat-tatting like hailstones on a corrugated roof. I peered round the slice of opening. It was as gloomy as a December evening. Where the boards outside had weather warped, shafts of light snuck through, shimmered like weak spotlights. I idled in the doorway, waited for my peepers to adjust to night vision. Whilst idling I caught the scent of beeswax, Brasso, weak disinfectant. Someone cared enough to keep the place clean. I wondered if it was Big Shirley, or maybe a weekly char.

At last I made sense of the shadows, picked out the shape of brown upholstered booths, the cast iron tables and chairs, the small yawn of empty stage. My feet took me further in, my hand dusted along the cherry wood bar, past the redundant beer pumps. The fine hairs on my arms stood to attention with military alertness. I frittered away some minutes remembering the last visit. The club was thick with smoke back then, the jukebox loud, trying its hardest to drown out the gossipers, the mourners, the sobbing that sometimes broke free on the recalling of memories. If I looked east I pictured Denny Doyle flirting with the tawny- haired girl.

Tipping my chin west I met the muddy browns belonging to Sullivan. I still saw danger, he still saw everything there was to see. In my mind I played that crooked smile of his, but it wasn't aimed at me. It was for Stella. She sidled up to him, mascara streaking her face. Of course now I fully understood the tears. They weren't just for Uncle Stavros, they were for herself too, for the baby growing in her belly. And there was Rita, at the table for two, stormy green eyes watching, waiting. The club was crowded with ghosts, all of them breathing. The ghost I most wanted to meet refused to put in an appearance.

At the end of the cherry wood I raised the hinged piece of bar, weaved around the furniture, scaled the pair of steps, stood center-stage. Again I frittered away time, imagined how it felt to be a performer, a singer like Big Shirley, or a dancer like Stella. I wondered if Dad did a turn in his heyday. A movement in the gloom ahead captured my attention. I caught a breath. The lungs held it in custody. I listened to my heart clatter out of control beneath my ribs.

"And now, ladies and gentlemen, for one night only, I give you the delicious, the delightful, the divine songbird, Little Miss Ruby."

I recognised the voice. A slow handclap echoed off the walls, a couple of wolf- whistles, chanting. *Ruby, Ruby, Ruby.* I considered my options. Two sprang to mind. My gut instinct favoured the first, do a flyer. Good job my head was on the level though, 'cos I was pretty sure my shoes were nail gunned to the boards. That left me with the second choice. I can assure you I wasn't exactly over the moon about it either. I geared myself up, remembered Frankie Doyle once said everyone had a talent waiting to be discovered. His was musical. He could play the guitar like a professional. I'd found that attractive, plus the fact he was a dead ringer for his brother Denny, my heart's desire, at least from a distance anyway.

He was also a lot kinder, told me he really really loved me, and I loved him, just not really really. Though for a while I pretended to. But that's the trouble with love on the rebound, isn't it?

Anyhow, for my second choice I decided to sing a song I never grew tired of hearing Frankie play. I filled the old air-bags, gave it my best shot. I sang of Mr Tambourine Man, of jingle- jangle mornings, of trips upon a magic swirling ship. And when I finished the adrenaline was fast flowing, and my smile was as wide as the Grand Canyon, and I wanted to do it all over again.

"Well, you can hold a tune, I'll give you that," the audience of one said. "Right regular little warbler, aren't you?"

I hitched a shoulder, peeled my soles off the floor, left the stage.

"What are you doing in here, Ruby girl?"

I walked til I reached the table with its lone occupier, sat, placed elbows on the cool cast iron, fixed my eyeballs on his, noted the irritated glint in them. Only the truth would keep him sweet.

"The door was open," I said, "so thought I'd take a look."

"Satisfied now then, are you?"

"No, not really, but I'll tell you something for nothing though. You nearly gave me a bloody heart attack."

He chuckled, turned his face to the stage again, puffed on a roll-up. I heard the crackle of burning baccy, smelled the familiar scent of Sun Valley.

"You won't find what you're looking for in here, me darlin'."

"I wasn't looking for anything, Dad."

"Weren't you, Ruby?"

"No, there's nothing to find in a closed down club, is there."

"What, not even a ghost?"

"I don't believe in ghosts. I'm not a kid anymore, you know, I'm nearly sixteen."

"We may as well leave then. Come on; let's go before Big Shirley sends out a search party."

I let him lead the way out. At the hinged piece of bar he waved me through, lowered it behind us, tracked me along the cherry wood to the heavy duty door. As he began to shut it I swear to God I heard Sinatra singing, heard him singing about the summer wind blowing in. I stood on tiptoe, peered over Dad's right shoulder. Dust motes were swirling as if they'd been disturbed.

19

I **took myself off** to bed early. Dad had cracked a bottle of Southern Comfort, was set on getting smashed. Big Shirley grated on my nerves doing a Charlie Drake impression. Much as I loved Mr Drake there's only so many 'hello my darlings' a girl can take, isn't there?

As usual, alongside the drinking of alcoholic beverages, came the reminiscing. For a while I listened with lugholes half alert, soon grew tired of hearing about rationing and doodlebugs, or the day the Yanks moseyed into town, bamboozling the dames with gifts of sheer nylons, leaving behind surprise babies and broken hearts. I recall Mum once saying a moment of madness was a costly affair. Vera said it took two to heat the sheets.

As far as I was concerned, all that was yesterday's news. Time had moved on. We were in the swinging sixties. Even if my estate wasn't yet that swinging, us kids were shrugging off those post-war straight-jackets, were ripe for a revolution, with fashion and music being our choice of weapon to carry us forward into battle.

There were rumblings too from women wanting liberation. Maureen from the Co-op said sisters should stand together, should remember what the likes of Mrs Pankhurst went through for us. Anyone with an ounce of know-how couldn't help but see the passion on her face, the fire in her eyes.

Her boyfriend Billy, the tattooed lorry driver, would smile the kind of smile that didn't quite make the grade. He reckoned women were fussing about sod all, they already had men by the short and curlies one way or another. Pity he didn't think before talking. It proved to be his loss in the long run. Mine too the day she finally freed herself of him.

Anyway, sick of hearing Big Shirley's voice, I left the pair of them to it. I had a plan to run through, hadn't come all this way just to perch on my derriere. For starters, there was Uncle Stavros' bedroom crying out for a drop in. Maybe a fresh set of peepers would see the overlooked obvious, like a written confessional, or even better the gun, 'cos lips were pressed tighter than a nun's knees on the circumstances of his untimely departure.

Gut feeling told me I hadn't heard the half of what happened that fateful day. I was big on gut feelings. Dad said it was the one thing you could trust a hundred per cent.

And now there was the singing ghost business. I knew it wasn't the real Sinatra, he was still alive and kicking. Not only that, I couldn't quite see him any time soon on some easy street in Soho. So I wondered if my Uncle had done a U-turn before reaching the spirit world, wondered if he was restless over the shortfall in justice over his ill-fated demise. I needed to talk to Big Shirley on her lonesome. If anyone knew anything about ghosts in the club it was bound to be her. Perhaps that was the benefit Dad got for her living there rent free. Perhaps she kept Uncle's soul company 'til he could R.I.P. Or perhaps I'd picked up Mr Doyle's gift, could receive messages from the other side. It didn't appeal to me as much I'd thought, and I'll tell you why. Nobody in their right mind wants to be known as the local fruit and nut case, do they? Only the likes of Mr Doyle can wear that title with some degree of comfort.

I slipped into my nightie with the embroidered red rosebuds. Although the hour was late, the sky outside was lit by a neon sign. Hot pink and dragonfly blue brushed the bedroom walls. I found that agreeable, seeing as the dark and I weren't compatible. To be on the safe side I decided to leave the door ajar as well. A wedge of gold cut across the carpet. I heard Big Shirley start a song. There was a big fanfare before she told us day-o, daylight had come and she wanted to go home. Dad filled in the backing.

It was clear I'd get precious little shut-eye with her in such fine fettle, snuggled between crisp cotton sheets anyway, tugged the lemon candlewick bedspread under my chin, dropped the blinkers over my peepers. I heard the sound of distant stilettos tapping. As they click-clacked nearer a soprano giggled invitingly. A baritone responded, his laugh charged with expectation. The tapping stilettos continued on, faded away. I wondered if she'd risk stepping over the line of decency tonight.

A car rumbled by, someone running, footfalls smacking the pavement. Big Shirley finished the song. Dad clapped, whistled. She said, "How's about you doing a turn, Mickey, for old time's sake, eh?"

My blinkers rolled up. I flung back the bedcovers, planted my tootsies on the floor, waited on Dad's reply. Seconds passed. I stood, padded to the window, pressed my brow against the cool glass, stared at the neon sign opposite. The silhouette of a naked lady flashed hot pink, teasing, now you see me, now you don't. The name *Delilah* in dragonfly blue sprawled beneath her. It told me exactly what sort of place it was, the sort of place Vera called all tits and tassels.

"Yeah, why don't I, my friend." A glass thumped on wood.

"So what will you sing?" Big Shirley sounded impatient.

"Jesus, give me a chance to decide, will you?"

"I'm excited is all, Mickey. You haven't sung in ages here. It'll be like the good old days, won't it?"

There was a wistful tone to her voice. I raised my peepers to heaven. In my opinion the good old days were far too over-rated. I'd earwigged on enough grievances to know how hard they'd had it, what with the blackouts and bombings, the women forever more in mourning for their menfolk. I couldn't see much good in that little lot.

"The good old days are gone, Shirley," Dad said.

"And don't I know it. You singing or not, Mickey, 'cos I've another number I'm itching to do if you're not fussed?"

"Yeah, I'm singing."

I tipped my left lughole to the door on the jar. Of course I'd heard Dad sing before. Sometimes he joined in with the radio. Sometimes, if the yen took him, he'd hammer away at the old upright, belt out a tune or two. Sometimes he put so much feeling into the words I came over all emotional. In anticipation I found my breathing grew shallow, my heart began beating as loud as crashing cymbals. And then he sang the first line. Big Shirley supplied the harmonies. Chills skittered up my spine, tingled the downy hair on the nape of my neck. Tears brimmed. I believed every word. Every catch in his voice caused a tightening in my throat. He sang about being the great pretender.

I faced the window again. The naked lady continued to flash. A group of six well-heeled men paused at the entrance of the strip-club. Somebody said, "Come on, boys, let's catch the last show."

The door opened. A snatch of raunchy music, heavy on the drums, made a bid for freedom. The men moved inside, laughing, back slapping, shoulder bumping. I supposed the trade in titillation was booming.

Mumblings from below told me the carousing was done with. I heard Dad softly whistling his way along the hall, guessed he was calling it a night. A gurgle of water hit the Butler sink, indicated Big Shirley was cleaning up. She wouldn't rest easy til everything was ship-shape. Maybe I should join her, indulge my need for a touch of interrogation whilst she was tongue-loose on Southern Comfort.

Pulling on my dressing-gown on I tippy-toed down the staircase just wide enough for one. A few steps more brought me to the kitchen. I peeped around the door frame. Big Shirley hummed as she swiped a dishcloth over already squeaky-clean surfaces. Two washed and dried tumblers squatted beside a near empty whiskey bottle. The sash window was hoisted north. A gentle breeze ruffled red gingham curtains, dragged in air layered with city smells, petrol fumes, late night fry-ups. Far flung voices shrieked like injured animals. I gave a polite ahem, smirked as she jumped out of her skin, gripped the sink for support.

"Holy Mother of God save us." She pressed a palm against her chest. "What the bloody hell are you playing at, creeping up on a person like that? You just scared me half to death."

I detected a slur. The booze had done its job. My smirk widened. It should be a piece of cake winkling out the information with her in such a state of picklement. I high-stepped it deeper into the kitchen, smelled the scent of Fairy washing-up liquid. She rolled canary yellow Marigolds off her hands. The snap of rubber as they released their hold sounded like the crack of a gunshot. I met her bleary eyeball with a cocksure one of my own.

"Jesus, I need a drink." She up-ended the near empty bottle, necked it neat. The dregs of Southern Comfort vanished in three glugs. I watched her Adam's apple bob in her throat with each swallow. Peeling back her lips she hissed out a breath between clenched teeth. I noticed they were small, a shade barely short of snowy-white.

"I'd have thought you'd guzzled enough of that already," I said, followed it up with a sniff full of disdain.

"Yeah, that's what I thought 'til my whole life flashed before my eyes, thanks to you."

She walked a crooked path through the brick archway, took great care to place herself on a chair at the table. I followed, chose the seat alongside. "What are you doing here anyways, squirt?"

"I want to ask you something, Shirley." I settled myself in for the long haul.

"Well it's late and I'm afraid I've got myself intoxicated, so now's not the time for questions." She closed her left eye, kept the right one fixed on me, massaged her temples. I noticed her nails were painted crimson. It proved she hadn't completely given up on the Big Shirley I preferred.

"It's only one question, Shirley, that's all, I promise."

"Can't it wait 'til morning?" She yawned, circled her arms on the table, laid her head in the center. The aroma of stale whiskey wafted my way. A drool of spit pooled at the corner of her slack mouth. "I'm never going to drink again, squirt. It's bloody horrible."

I snorted, raised my eyebrows. I'd heard that said plenty before, except from Vera, of course. She wouldn't dare say it, not when it was common knowledge her day started with a vodka breakfast and Trebor extra strong mints.

I lowered my face to Big Shirley's level. Both eyes were closed. I observed well-used laughter lines, cheeks marred with strawberry coloured thread veins. Purple shadows underlined dark lashes. With the pad of my thumb, I lifted an eyelid. The pupil shrank under the battering of the electric light. She made a feeble attempt at resistance. And then I had a thought. Where was Big Shirley the night my Uncle took the fatal bullet? I sat up straight.

"Where were you, Shirley, on the night of the shooting?" My voice came out as a whisper. I hadn't wanted it to, and I already knew the answer, she had been there too, Black Jack wasn't the only witness. Maybe there were more. Maybe Rita, or Abraham Golding, the TCP man. But one thing I knew for certain. Black Jack had the gun. I'd seen it.

"Leave me be, Ruby, I don't want to remember."

Unfortunately she hadn't a hope in that hot place called hell of me leaving her alone. I lifted an eyelid again.

"You were there, weren't you, Shirley? So was Black Jack. And now he's missing. Only the guilty goes on the run. You know that much, same as I do."

Her eyeball sought me out, made a mess of focusing. My heart thundered beneath my ribs like a stampeding herd of buffalo across the prairie. I could almost taste the dust they kicked up. But Shirley wasn't the patsy I'd thought she was.

"I know what you're after, Ruby Blackbee." She raised herself upright, pulled a pack of filter-free Players from her trousers pocket, shook one out. She struck a match. I watched the flame burn blue, turn yellow. I smelled the sulphur as she lit the gasper.

"I'm only after the truth, Shirley. That's all." I too straightened up.

"Then ask your father for it."

"He won't talk. No-one will. They treat me like a kid."

"That's 'cos you are a kid." Her voice grew soft. "You're best off staying that way for as long as you can, squirt. Trust me; it ain't half as much fun being a grown-up."

"Please, Shirley, just tell me what happened." Even though she didn't move a muscle I could sense her drawing away from me. Soon I would lose her altogether. "I know you were there. I know Jack made my Uncle play Russian roulette. He as good as murdered him, didn't he?"

I studied her face. If my take on that night hit a nerve I was sure to see a sign. Perhaps she'd refuse to look me in the eye. Perhaps she'd purse her lips tight to stop them spilling the beans. She did neither. Instead she leaned forward til her nose near on touched the tip of mine. Smoke lingered on her breath. I refused to back off. She'd only take it as a weakness.

"Now why would he do that, eh, Ruby?"

"'Cos he's crazy, that's why. He tried to run me over once, as well. That's how crazy he is, stark raving bonkers."

"That's not the way I heard it, squirt. I heard you stepped off the kerb without checking the coast was clear, took a bash and thought Jesus had paid you a personal visit."

"And he has a gun. I saw it, last New Year's Eve. I saw it with my own eyes."

"You saw nothing, do you hear me?" She moved her nose away. I grabbed her hand before she could move the rest of her.

"But am I right, Shirley? Is Jack crazy enough to murder?"

"You couldn't be more wrong if you tried." She slipped her hand from my grasp, got to her feet. I raised my chin, looked her square in the eye. She returned an icy stare. "Now leave me alone. I'm tired."

I watched her totter towards the brick arch, remembered the singing ghost. As I'm a selfish no good for nothing whatsit I said, "Have you heard the singing ghost then, Shirley?"

She stopped in her tracks, glanced over her left shoulder. I caught the tail-end of a smile.

"What do you reckon? Sweet dreams, squirt, night-night, sleep tight."

She disappeared. I sat for a few minutes more, putting my thoughts in order. If there was a chance, however slim in my opinion, that Black Jack wasn't involved, who else was there? Nobody sprang to mind, only more loose ends. I flicked the lights off, made my way to the bedroom under the eaves.

"Don't let the bedbugs bite," I said.

20

The whistling of Moon River roused me from my slumber. I split apart my eyelids. Soft light broke through the curtains. For a while I listened to the sounds of a new morning.

Outside cars trundled by. A horn blasted. Another answered with a couple of short angry honks. Muted chit-chat filtered up from the street, some laughing. A man's voice shouted, "Jimmy, get over here, mate."

Inside I caught the whiff of bacon grilling, the aroma of boiling water over instant coffee, heard the rattle of a spoon against china. All that kind of let slip I had slept too long, wouldn't be checking out Uncle's bedroom tucked under the eaves in the foreseeable future.

With a mood on me as dark as an unlit sky, I joined Dad and Big Shirley in the kitchen.

"Hooray," Dad said, "Sleeping Beauty awakes."

"I seriously doubt there's a Prince Charming brave enough to wake this particular Sleeping Beauty, Mickey," Big Shirley said.

I snarled, shuffled through the brick arch, sat opposite Big Shirley at the table. She seemed in bad shape. Bloodshot eyes clashed with an emerald wrap over-indulged with spangles. I thought the material could be silk, took a fistful, caressed it between my fingertips. It didn't feel slinky, guessed it was imitation, same as everything else about her.

She hissed at me like Monty the marmalade cat. Her breath smelled worse than the creek at low tide on a sunny day. I turned my hooter east, gave Dad a tortured look. He placed a heap of hot bacon butties between us, a mug of steaming black coffee, a cup of milky tea for me.

Big Shirley grimaced, turned a shade of frog green. I sniggered, selected a butty, worked it over with my molars. Melted butter dripped down my chin. I swiped at it with a sleeve, grinned at her with mouth crammed to capacity.

"You're disgusting, you are." She sniffed, sipped the coffee, offered me the cold shoulder. "You've raised a proper brat, Mickey Blackbee, and no mistaking."

"Yeah, I know she is," Dad said. "As soon as breakfast is done I'm going to beat seven bales out of her."

I cast my peepers to the ceiling, continued chewing. I'd heard that empty threat plenty of times before. When my sight levelled, I noticed Dad's face was freshly de-whiskered. His shirt had the top button popped, the tie was loosened off. Then I remembered the reason we were there, for the meeting with Mr Shuffles to decide the fate of the baby with no name. I stopped chewing. The on-set of jitters shaved the edge right off my appetite. I struggled to drag air down to the lungs, wondered how long a heart could survive without oxygen, pressed an open palm to my chest. It was still ticking.

"So, how did the meeting with Shuffles go?" Big Shirley saved me from asking the most important question of the day. Whilst waiting on the answer she searched in the robes pocket, fished out a crumpled pack of gaspers. She shook out a Players, tossed it across the table to Dad, shook out another for herself. They lit them in unison, drew in long and deep. Big Shirley snorted smoke through her nostrils. Dad blew a chain of perfect rings. Whorls of grey spiralled upwards, rolled around the glass chandelier.

"Well, I went to that dump he calls an office dead on nine as agreed, and guess what he tells me, Shirley?" Dad pushed the fingers of his left hand through his hair, scratched the nape of his neck.

"I don't know, Mickey. What did he tell you?"

"He tells me Stella's already paid him a visit last week."

My belly danced the bossa nova. Stella was in Soho, had realised she'd made a grave error of judgement, wanted her son back where he belonged. Any minute soon I hoped to hear the good news. The baby with no name was leaving.

Naturally Mum would be devastated. A small pang of regret on her behalf stabbed at the few scruples I owned. I imagined how her empty arms would ache, how the tears would fall when she thought the rest of us were in the land of nod. But Dad and I would be wide awake, waiting for the sound of weeping 'cos we'd know it was due, we'd know her heart was breaking in two.

Only Granny Bee, who wasn't fully switched on anymore, would be oblivious, would be snoring open-mouthed as usual, her gnashers wrapped in a clean hankie beneath her pillow. And, needless to say, Monty the cat, curled nose to tail on the end of the bed. Unless he was hunting. On those nights Granny perched on the brown wing-back chair, peering out the bedroom window for him to come moseying home. When she heard the jingle of the bell attached to his collar she'd unlock the latch, call him up. He'd use the metal dustbin and outside lavvy roof as a ladder, before making a short leap in through the opening.

Sometimes, if I wasn't properly asleep, I'd hear the jingle too, the thud of Monty's paws, Granny's low murmur of welcome. Sometimes, if I bothered to look out my window, I'd see Steven Shaw, the ex-POW from next door, prowling the garden fence. On those nights I guessed his mind had taken him back in time, back to his friend Sonny Jim, back to a place where unspeakable things happened.

Anyway, I don't mind admitting I hated Stella right then. I hated her for leaving that baby with us, for making even me feel something bordering on affection for him.

"Christ, she's got some brass on her, hasn't she, Mickey?" Big Shirley said.

"Not really, Shirley. What she's done must have almost killed her." Dad took a last drag, stubbed out the dog-end, gazed at a black and white print of matchstick men hanging skew-whiff on the far wall.

"What she's done is break poor Joanie's heart." Big Shirley's voice sounded snappy.

I folded arms across my chest, nodded agreement. Tilting my chin west I gifted Dad with a glare fit for the traitor he'd turned out to be, could hardly believe he'd found a shred of sympathy for that strumpet Stella, especially after all the hurt she was about to cause again.

After all, if it wasn't for her and my uncle doing the horizontal tango there'd be no baby to haggle over. If it weren't for them I wouldn't have heard the singing ghost, or seen the swirling dust motes, or gone and dumped myself in a whole heap of doodah with Mum. I still had her to contend with. There'd be no baby to soften the blow now, would there? And worse than that, I still had the pain of one of Vera's famous Chinese burns to look forward to.

"No, Shirley, she's more than likely broken her own heart," Dad said.

"What do you mean by that?" Big Shirley flashed the fags again, offered one to Dad.

He declined, paced to the matchstick men, straightened the frame, made a return. His hands beat a drum roll on the table.

"The baby stays with us, my old fruit, that's what I mean."

I wailed like a violin out of tune. It was bad news. Of course Mum would be happy. And even though I wasn't feeling the joy, I could tolerate a small discrepancy of that sort. It wasn't her fault the maternal instincts were stronger than her common sense. And it wasn't written in the Gospel I'd be required to help raise the baby. Anyway, I'd be far too busy for him to bother me much. I had dreams to follow, Denny Doyle to nail down.

"Holy Moses, Mickey." Big Shirley clapped, scraped back her chair, stood, danced a jig. "Joanie will be beside herself. Is it legal though? "

"As legal as it can be. There are certain conditions though," Dad said.

"Oh here we go, complications more likely, eh, Mickey. Knew it was too good to be true. Nothing's that simple anymore is it?"

"It's only a couple of points, Shirley." Dad moved to the window that overlooked the small garden for punters to enjoy if the weather allowed, the private bricked off yard done out in concrete. I knew exactly what he could see. To the left three trestle tables and six bench seats, in urgent need of a brush of creosote, circled a blooming lilac tree. I wondered how many backsides had polished those smooth slats, wondered how many promises were made under the influence of a pint and whiskey chaser, how many broken under the cold sober light of dawn.

On the right a grey plastic donkey stood lonely in the concrete yard. The baskets slung across it's flanks were trailing with flowering cherry coloured geraniums. I supposed keeping things half together was also part of the deal for Big Shirley living there rent free.

"What're those so called certain conditions then?" Big Shirley yawned. I noticed her molars didn't hold a single filling. She stretched. The edges of her emerald wrap parted company. Maroon paisley pyjamas were put on display.

"It's nothing major." Dad shrugged.

My peepers drilled into the space between his shoulder blades. The outline of a vest showed through his white cotton shirt. He always wore a vest, reckoned it kept the cold out and the heat in. If the day was a scorcher he peeled off the shirt. If Mum was present he grinned and flexed his muscles. She'd laugh, wait for what was coming next, to be scooped up as if she weighed nothing. She'd link her arms around his neck, call him a fool. When I was young I'd whine for a turn. Sometimes he'd spin in circles 'til we were both giddy, falling over drunk. Sometimes he tipped me upside down. It hadn't happened in a long while. At fifteen and three quarters I thought I'd probably outgrown those kinds of high jinks'. Trouble was, remembering made me miss them all the more.

"Righty-ho, then, let's shape up and ship out." Dad peeled himself away from the view. "Get your things together, Ruby, I'm leaving in ten minutes."

"Oh thank the good Lord for small mercies," Big Shirley said. "I'll be glad to see the back of you both."

I set my kisser into a sneer, opened my mouth ready to reel off a smart-alecky reply. Luckily I caught the look Dad and Big Shirley traded. It was the type of look I'd seen before, the type grown-ups give when there's more to say, just not in my company. So I slid of the chair, made a show of a downtrodden departure. Once out of sight I stalled behind the kitchen door, lugholes primed. I wasn't disappointed. And I knew who they were talking about.

"Did you make those phone calls this morning, Shirley?" Dad said.

"Yeah, words out he's around," Big Shirley said.

"Still alive then."

"Struggling though, if the gossip's true, Mickey."

"Find him, Shirley, pull out all the stops. Just do whatever it takes."

"It's not easy tracking down an old soldier if he don't want to be found. You know that better than anyone."

"Yeah, and he was one of the best."

The chink of china being stacked warned me I'd best scoot. I made it safe to the bedroom under the eaves before I heard Dad's dulcet tones.

"Five minutes, Ruby, before I'm gone. Be ready, else it's a long walk home."

I stuffed the nightie with the red embroidered rosebuds into the brown leather holdall. My dressing-gown followed. I dragged a comb through my tangled hair, threw it on top, zipped the zipper, vacated the room, battled down the staircase only wide enough for one, found Big Shirley leaning against the white glossed banisters.

"So, how you doing, squirt?" she said.

"Fantastic." I stretched the word out as far as it would go.

"Got yourself a boyfriend yet?"

"Hundreds of them." I dropped the holdall to the floor, shoved it with my right foot.

We watched it tumble over the steps, roll to a stop on the chequered floor tiles.

"'Course you have." Her lips spread. The smile fell short of reaching the eyes. "It'll all work out in the end, Ruby girl, it always does."

"Fat chance of that happening," I said. "We've got baby for a reminder, haven't we?"

Big Shirley's hands moved faster than a striking snake. Strong fingers gripped my collar bones. She leaned into my face. The smell of her breath hadn't improved. I inhaled day old fermented whiskey fumes.

"It will work out, I promise." She folded me into a two armed hug.

"It won't, Shirley." I said against her ribcage. "There's too many secrets nobody wants to talk about."

I heard the whisper of a sigh escape her lungs, felt warm air upon my head. She hugged tighter.

"Oh Ruby, some things are really best left unsaid. Now get out of here, before your father buggers off without you." She held me at arm's length. "That would ruin my day, that would, squirt, having to put up with you any longer than necessary."

"Yeah, and I'd rather risk hitching a lift with the Ripper than listen to you slaughter another Bassey number."

I started down the stairs. On the bottom step I glanced over my shoulder. Big Shirley had gone. My peepers flicked to the Club door. Perhaps it was still unlocked. If by any slim piece of luck it was, perhaps I'd hear the soft singing again, see the dust motes swirling as if they'd been disturbed. Then I'd know for sure the ghost I loved the most was sending me a sign. Then I'd have a private word with Mr Doyle, 'cos he talked to dead people. I shifted my black slip-ons forward.

"If you've finished saying your au revoirs, Ruby, I'd like to get rolling along the tarmac." Dad's voice put the brakes on my intentions.

"I've finished," I said, "and if I never see Shirley again it'll be too soon."

"How nice." I detected a flavour of sarcasm from him, decided to ignore it. He tucked the holdall under his armpit, spared me five seconds of the beady eye, walked out the front door. I followed, slammed the wood in the hole, parked myself on the passenger seat, twiddled with the tuner on the radio. Ringo began the story about a yellow submarine. Dad slid in the driver's side, cranked the engine, twiddled with the tuner too. Connie Francis told me stupid cupid was a real mean guy. I should have taken notice of her.

We drove home. Conversation was pretty scarce between us. As I'm not a fan of the silence my nerves were wound tighter than the strings on Frankie's guitar. Dad took the sharp corner into Nickle Street too fast, tucked our Ford Estate behind a Volkswagen camper. The exhaust belched puffs of black smoke, the body was done over in many shades of hand- painted flowers. It took a bit of searching to discover the colour of the original spray job.

The van stalled outside number twenty-three. Dad parked opposite, left the engine ticking over. We stared across the street, didn't have long to wait before a vision of loveliness made an appearance.

"Bloody Nora." Dad killed the engine, got out the car. I joined him on the pavement.

We stood side by side, me admiring the vision of loveliness, him fixing a roll-up. I heard the drone of a lone bee busy gathering nectar. "What the hell is that?"

"A Hippy," I said, "a free spirit."

"A free spirit?" He took a drag, snorted out smoke. Going on the tone of his voice, I half expected flames of fire to follow. "Bloody free-loader more like."

"Oh Dad." I sighed, beefed it up with a tut. "It's all about love, about anti-war."

"Anti-war?" I could almost hear his teeth grinding. "Good job we didn't all think that in '39, isn't it? Bloody anti-work, I reckon."

"You just don't understand, Dad." My peepers performed a 360° rotation. When they eventually re-focused, I discreetly slid them west across the street, helped myself to another butchers of the real live Hippy. He'd slipped on shades with blue lenses. His lips were full and slightly parted. A lazy smile tugged the corners of his mouth. He flashed the peace salute. I saluted back. My heart produced a flawless somersault. I heard the twang as Cupid fired off a dart. Not even a bulletproof vest could have saved me.

21

"**B**ring the bags in, Ruby girl," Dad said. "I'll go ahead, soften your mother up with the good news. If you're lucky she won't ground you for the rest of your natural life."

I watched him move his heels along the garden path, listened to the whistle on his lips. It took a moment before I placed the tune. Then I could almost hear Ray Charles begging that poor woman he'd grown tired of to take those chains from his heart and set him free.

I returned my attention back to the vision of loveliness, committed everything about him to memory, the corn coloured hair, the faded low-slung jeans, the tan moccasins. I took some time giving him the once over, wondered how those plump lips would feel against mine. And then without as much as a backwards glance he vanished through the side gate of number twenty-three. And I got on with the job of manhandling that hefty brown leather holdall to our front door.

The midday sun burned high in a cloudless sky. Windows were swung open. A gentle breeze dragged the curtains to and fro. Radios were blaring. Kids were whining. Women were gassing. Dusty began a lament about wishing and hoping. I did too. I wished and hoped the news concerning the baby with no name would spare me a grounding. I must have wished and hoped hard enough 'cos the sound of snivelling filtered along the hall. It was a positive sign. It meant Mum was in an emotional state. My latest shenanigans wouldn't be top priority. It might even be safe to show my face. So I chanced it. I sidestepped into the kitchen, leaned against the larder door. The scene was just as I expected. Dad fixed a gasper. Mum was blotting her eyes. Granny Bee cradled the baby, warbled some beef about a sailor, some plea for him to stop his roaming. Vera flitted around putting a brew together. I noticed her hands were shaking worse than usual. That indicated she'd probably overindulged on the Russian nectar again, would need to cut back before she tipped over the edge, required a period of drying out. To confirm my suspicions she fetched the small silver hipflask from her handbag, swigged a long shot down her throat. Yes, it was a dead cert that pretty soon she'd fall apart, would take refuge in our dossers bedroom for waifs and strays and down and outs. It would be hell, especially for Mum who'd have to deal with her, bully her, plead with her, wash her hair, near enough force feed her, else she'd waste away on a diet of Woodbines and endless cups of tea. Not so much hell for me. When Vera suffered one of these episodes she was inclined to grow a trifle lip loose, was inclined to let slip a secret or two. And as I'm a mercenary little maggot I planned on being there, to steer her intoxicated memories towards Black Jack, to hear exactly what he'd meant to her back in the days of long ago. And, more importantly, if he was the murdering son of a gun I thought he was.

"Oh God, Mickey," Mum said. "I can hardly believe he's here to stay. Tell me again, Mickey, tell me everything again. I just can't take it all in. It's nothing short of a miracle, that's what it is. I didn't think I'd see the day I'd hold another baby in my arms."

I swivelled my peepers east towards Dad. His showed no sign of emotion. His eyes stayed as cool as always. He ran the fingers of his right hand through his hair, left it standing on end. An image of Ken Dodd and his tickling stick came uninvited to my mind.

"He stays," he said, "but there are a couple of conditions I agreed to."

"Conditions, Mickey?"

I heard the concern in Mum's question, swivelled my peepers west, saw it clearly marked on her face, the raised eyebrows, the unblinking stare, the unspoken demand for an answer.

"It's just a couple of things, Joan, nothing to worry yourself about."

I heard the resignation in Dad's answer. He knew as well as me what was coming next.

"So what are these couple of things then, Mickey, the ones with nothing to worry about?"

I sighed. The concern had definitely turned tail, chased away by wariness, and something else, something like disappointment.

"Shall we talk later about this, Joan, when we're alone?" Dad nodded in my direction, swigged the dregs of his tea, rose from his chair, settled his cap upon his head, made to leave.

"No, we shan't talk later, Mickey." Mum crossed arms under her ample bosom, her favourite position for the onset of battle. Or perhaps it'd be the usual skirmish. Really depended on the strength of Dad's resistance. "I'm not waiting a minute longer. I need to know exactly where we stand, exactly what those foolhardy so called conditions you've saddled us with are. Did you not even consider discussing this with me, Mickey Blackbee? Seems you're getting far too fond of making the decisions around here lately, in my opinion, so out with it, before you live to regret the day we met."

"For God's sake, Joan, how the hell could I discuss it with you?" He returned his backside to the chair, slapped his cap on the table. "What did you expect me to do? Send a note by pigeon post? Or maybe a smoke signal? Jesus, woman, you're enough to try the patience of a saint."

A smile twitched the corners of my mouth. Obviously the strength of his resistance was high that day. If Mum didn't take care, those couple of conditions wouldn't be forthcoming any time soon. But, of course, she knew her husband better than he knew himself. I've noticed that about canny women. They have ways and means, don't they? And secret promises shared with a certain look, a look that suggests a trip to paradise isn't far off if the man of their hearts desire plays his cards right. On occasion I've practised that certain look on Denny Doyle, my own heart's desire, sadly without success. Maybe he hadn't yet learned to read the message behind a certain look. But then again he didn't need to, did he? All the girls within a two mile radius were giving him the barefaced come-on. Messages behind their certain looks didn't need code cracking. Denny Doyle was spoiled for choice. And I didn't seem to be a choice he'd thought of considering.

"Mickey." Mum scooped the baby with no name from Granny Bee's arms. Monty the marmalade cat took advantage, settled on the warmth of her lap, pummelled her spare tyres with outstretched claws. She smoothed a palm over his back. He purred his appreciation. "Just tell me, Mickey, please, let's get it over and done with."

Vera fussed around refilling cups with half stewed tea. I stayed propping up the larder door, as still and quiet as I possibly could be, hardly daring to breath, praying I wouldn't be noticed, be sent on my way whilst more secrets were aired then stored, never to see the light of day again. Only my lugholes were silently flapping.

"Please, Mickey," Mum said. "I need to know."

I watched Dad build a roll-up, stir two sugars into his half stewed tea, flick the little wheel on the Ronson lighter, set the baccy afire. I inhaled the aroma of lighter fuel, the scent of Sun Valley.

"All right, Joan," Dad said, "but before you go for the jugular, let me finish talking."

"Of course I will." Mum exercised a slow motion eye roll. "Good God, what do you take me for, Mickey Blackbee? Anyone would think I never let you finish a bloody sentence, wouldn't they?" She turned to Vera. "For goodness sakes, have you ever heard the like, my friend? Tell him not to be so ridiculous."

I exercised an eye roll manoeuvre of my own. When they eventually stopped rolling they got busy interpreting the faces present. Dad's was blank, Granny Bee's more so. No surprise there considering she was rarely fully engaged in the here and now. But Vera's face was loaded with doubt. Her raised eyebrows rippled her forehead. Her lips tried their best to find some words. The generous intake of vodka that day clearly dared her mouth to dispute the blatant bending of the truth.

"Well." Dad supped his tea, grimaced. "I went to old Shuffles office as arranged, and to cut a long story short, Stella had already been to see him, said she knew I'd be turning up sooner or later, and had an agreement she wanted signing concerning this baby here."

"She always was a sly fox, that one," Vera said.

"So, Joan, the choice was to sign and abide by the agreement, or not sign, and the baby would be placed in a children's home and put up for adoption. Think about that, Joan, when I tell you what these couple of conditions are, and you best be bleeding thankful I did sign and swear on the Holy Bible, 'cos you wouldn't be cradling that boy right now, this very minute, would you?" He threw her one of his dead in the tracks look. Although I only witnessed the look from the sidelines, I still felt the force of anger in it, saw the frayed edges of raw grief still festering. I glanced at Mum. She pulled herself up straighter, pushed back her shoulders, tightened her hold on the baby, raised her chin, gave him an unblinking stare.

"Go on then, Mickey," she said. "Let's hear it."

My peepers returned towards Dad. He held her stare for far longer than necessary. With every passing second the strain became as taut as the skin stretched over a snare drum. I felt the urge to scream. Fortunately, Vera chose that moment to clear her throat, rattle her cup on its saucer, break the spell of silence.

"First condition, Stella wants one photograph of the boy, taken on his birthday, sent to Shuffles and he'll forward it on to her."

"Well, that's very reasonable," Vera said.

"She wants no other contact, no letters, no phone calls, no nothing," Dad continued, "just the one photo."

"Bloody hell, as if we'd want any contact, eh?" Vera sniffed, balanced a

Woodbine between her lips. I noticed the Rimmel red was badly smudged at the right hand corner. "Caused enough mayhem here, hasn't she, without us going off searching for some more of the same?"

"Oh shut up, Vera," Mum said. "And for God's sake lay off that bloody juice. Haven't I enough to do without babysitting you through a drunken stupor? Go on, Mickey. What's the second thing?"

"His name, Joan." Dad re-lit his roll-up, gave it three quick drags. "The boy is to be called Andreas."

"Oh Lord." Vera's voice was barely a whisper. "He told her, didn't he? He told her about the Greek."

I'm pretty certain that time in our kitchen stopped for several heartbeats. Nobody so much as twitched a muscle. My peepers observed three other sets of peepers search each other out, share unspoken words, before settling en masse upon Granny Bee. I settled mine upon her as well and waited. And whilst waiting I saw Granny Bee's eyes clear, I saw a love in them, and her mouth became a smile, a smile so joyful my mouth smiled too.

And she said, "Andreas? My Andreas? Is he found?" And she looked for the answer from each face in turn. And I swear the years had rolled off her face, the creases smoothed out, the pale colour of her skin bloomed a delicate rose blush, and the beauty she used to be was briefly there again.

Of course it was Mum who eventually took charge. She laid the baby now with a name in Dad's arms, paced the few steps to sit beside Granny Bee.

"Not yet, Duchess, not yet." She smoothed the palm of her right hand across Granny Bee's left cheek.

And I witnessed that joyful smile tremble, witnessed the love in her eyes turn to pain.

"Where can he be, Joanie? He promised to come back for me."

And I remembered an earwigging incident, the one about people disappearing. And concrete boots. And food for the fishes. And I don't mind admitting my heart took a hit of that same pain. A solitary tear broke free from my left peeper. I let it run, felt its warmth as it tracked it's way south. And I thought, even if your mind was muddled like Granny Bee's, some memories just refuse to stay lost, don't they?

22

I'd like to tell you that we all lived happily ever after. I won't, of course, 'cos though I may be a lot of things most unsavoury, I'm not an out and out liar. And though Granny Bee was still a huge irritant, after the Andreas the Greek sailor incident I found myself slightly more tolerant of the cranky old gal. Even the very smallest dose of sympathy sometimes came a- tapping lightly upon my heart. And now she took to waiting at the front gate. Waiting and watching. Once I heard her softly call "Andreas, Andreas", heard the heavy burr on the letter R. How could you not be moved to tears occasionally?

Mum fussed, said it was a bloody sorry state of affairs. She worried too that Granny Bee might start wandering again. The first time it happened the milkman delivered her home with three pints of gold top. Dad set to, installed foolproof locks on the doors. But I suspect she must have been a safe-cracker in a previous life for it didn't take her long to crack the workings of a foolproof lock. Since then the coalman's twice dumped her next to the coal hole along with a sack of the usual. And a number of neighbours have returned her to the safe side of the gate. Lately though, she was content to just wait and watch for her lost love.

Dad found a battered wooden chair, glossed it red, set it on four grey paving slabs acquired from the local Council. And there she sat for hours on end if the weather was fine. On other days she'd twitch the curtains at the front window in the dossers room.

Anyway, Granny Bee's lost sailor, the baby Andreas, Vodka Vera's overindulgence of the white spirit weren't my main concern. Much to my delight I'd made progress on the romance front, was spending time in the company of Nick the Hippy, trading furtive glances, here and there a secret smile. Unfortunately, practically everyone else wanted to spend time with him too. And I'll tell you why. He had dreams we'd never thought of dreaming for ourselves. Of course being half Polish with that ever so slight accent he'd inherited from his father did him a pretty good turn. And so did the unproven rumour that Mr. Jankowski had seen the war out as a fighter pilot with Squadron 303 somewhere in Wiltshire. The patriotic blood still stirred in any living being who'd survived those years. It has to be said, memories have a long life.

So, come most evenings, the passion wagon was jam packed tighter than sardines in a tin. Smokes were shared. The air turned a hazy blue with the sweet smell of aromatic herbs. Smiles became permanent face fixtures. Thighs pressed against thighs on the padded bench seats. Arms with nowhere else to go linked with others, or wrapped around shoulders. Frankie strummed the strings. Voices took to singing. Woodpecker cider was the usual refreshment, sometimes a bottle or two of cut price plonk. Even Maureen from the Co-op made a habit of dropping by, especially when her boyfriend Billy, the tattooed lorry driver, was on a long distance haul. Even Denny Doyle put his love life on hold for an hour or two once in a while. Even my best friend Grace and her squeeze Duffy spared a little of their togetherness to listen to Nick talk of peace rallies, his plan to up sticks, travel to San Francisco, hitch his wagon on the tail end of a love train. And I'll tell you something for nothing. I was going with him. He didn't know it yet, but I considered that a minor detail.

And then the skate bait Rosemary Collins threw a party, a fancy dress party.

It was late August. Most of us wouldn't be returning to school, would be starting apprenticeships, or dead-end jobs. That wasn't going to happen to me. I wasn't wasting my life in a two-bit town working the assembly line in some factory. Or tying myself to a husband who turned into his dad as soon as his slippers were under the table. I was destined to go on a hippy adventure to San Francisco, with Nick Jankowski.

Anyway, back to Rosemary's party. It was held in the Church hall for a small donation towards the new roof fund. By the time I arrived it was almost crammed to full capacity. Half were on invites, the others were gate-crashers. Girls had put in more effort to dress up. There were plenty of princesses, a good number of Tinkerbelles. I noticed Rosemary made a slightly trashy Cinderella. I was Snow White. The boys had hardly troubled themselves, a few Elvis wigs, half a dozen gorillas. Jeremy Baker was the exception. He looked splendid as Marilyn Monroe. We'd grown accustomed to his strange habits. Nobody was shocked when he made a grand entrance.

My peepers searched around for Nick. They found Denny Doyle first. I felt the usual attraction for him stir in my belly, felt the stab of jealousy when a red haired fairy sidled alongside, tapped him on the chest with her wand. He smoothed his right palm down her back, left it resting on her derriere. I continued scanning the room whilst the fab four encouraged us to twist and shout, finally tracked down Nick, as usual surrounded by disciples. I gave him the once-over. He'd come as himself. I hadn't expected anything else.

I wandered nearer, hovered on the fringe of his entourage, spied Maureen from the Co-op. Seemed she was everywhere I was lately. Or perhaps everywhere Nick was.

Rosemary's parents struggled to supervise. They fought a losing battle. The sound of laughter was ear splitting, the bouquet of knocked-off scent overpowering. The fruit punch doctored with budget gin didn't help. Nor did the whiskey smuggled in under jackets, secretly swigged in darkened corners. I dusted down my throat with a beaker of fruit punch, then another. Some genius cranked the record player full volume. The Troggs thought they loved their wild thing but wanted to know for sure.

I joined the masses on the small dance floor. Bodies bumped bodies. The place purred with forbidden pleasures. The Walker Brothers began to croon. Apparently the sun wasn't going to shine anymore. Party-goers coupled up, swayed to the music. I looked for Nick. He was cheek to cheek with Maureen from the Co-op. I reckoned the sun wouldn't be shining for me that evening either.

"Wanna dance?" said a voice in my left ear.

I tipped my chin west. My vision blurred a little before clearing. Frankie Doyle stood beside me. I checked him over. He'd come as himself too.

"Can you dance then?" I said.

"'Course I can," he said.

And as my options were as usual seriously limited, I slung an arm round his neck, pulled him close, looked him dead straight in the eyes. They were as dark as Bournville chocolate.

"Let's dance," I said.

"Jesus, Ruby." Frankie's arms circled around me. "You been at that fruit punch?"

"What if I have?" I settled my head on his left shoulder, breathed in the scent of him.

He smelled freshly laundered. I took another sniff, picked up the aroma of Vosene shampoo, Imperial Leather soap. His black hair was as straight as Denny's was curly. He wore it Beatle style.

"Your dad's going to kill you." He sighed, tightened his hold on me.

I sighed, felt his lips brush a soft kiss upon my brow. I really liked Frankie and his gentle ways, his kindness. Right then I really wished I loved him, that fanfare and fireworks kind of love. I knew he'd treat me good. Problem was I doubted if I'd return the favour.

A scuffle on the outskirts caught my attention. Denny Doyle and another youth were squaring up. The distressed red haired fairy shifted herself a few paces south. Half a dozen other fairies rushed to her rescue, fussed around her like a clutch of clucking old hens. I wondered if it was satisfying for the ego to be fought over. I wondered if I'd ever have a chance to find out.

I forced my peepers to roam the Church Hall. They betrayed me, picked out Nick the Hippy, zoomed in on him faster than a Bazooka rocket I'd heard Dad talk about from his war days. He was still in a clinch with Maureen from the Co-op. They looked very much an item. My plan of riding on the tail end of a love train in San Francisco seemed pretty shakey. The boo-hoos threatened to break loose. I tilted my head, took a good long gander at Frankie. He gandered back. And I'll tell you something for free. I saw him in a different light. And the longer my peepers stayed on his, the brighter that light shone.

"Frankie," I said, "I want you to kiss me like Bogart kisses Bacall."

He took his time considering my request. It took me less than five seconds to surrender to that irksome impatience I'm far too familiar with.

"Well?" I said.

"Ruby, don't." His voice was low. I hesitated, thought I'd heard a faint warning tone about it, decided that would be ridiculous, so mistook it as a challenge instead.

"Don't what, Frankie?" I pushed my face closer, pressed my mouth against his, tasted whiskey, tasted the moan that escaped his throat, tasted the thrill of feeling wanted, of feeling desired.

That's when I let myself be led away. We weaved between the writhing bodies on the dance floor, snuck through the unmanned door. It was a beautiful August night. The heavens were littered with silver stars. A sultry breath of air lightly touched my skin. Frankie led me round to the back of the hall, pulled me down. I offered no resistance, laid upon the clover upholstered grass. The muffled sound of music drifted free from inside. Mr. McKenzie suggested that if we go to San Francisco we wear flowers in our hair. I wanted to go.

"Are you sure about this, Ruby?" Frankie said.

"I'm sure," I said.

And at that moment in time I was sure. At that moment in time I was reckless to the consequences on two beakers of doctored fruit punch. And with the lemon moon as my witness, Frankie, whispering words of love, showed me what fits where. That was the day I left home as pure as Snow White, and returned as shameless as a Jezebel.

23

"**Ruby,**" **Mum said,** "what are you doing mooching around the house again?"

I raised a shoulder, let it drop, said, "Nothing," slid on to a kitchen chair, put elbows on table, cupped my chin between palms. Truth was, after the sins of the flesh incident, I was avoiding Frankie Doyle. And I'll tell you why. What if he thought I was his girl now, that we were a couple fated to settle down to the mundane, to grow old together? He might be content to do just that, but I wasn't. Truth was I wanted nothing to do with the mundane, still harboured hopes of the San Francisco love train. And not only that, I wasn't sure if Frankie had taken me to heaven and back like Maureen from the Co-op said would happen.

"Jesus, couldn't get you to spend five minutes in at one time, could I, always in a hurry to be someplace else." Mum switched off the gas ring, silenced the whistler, poured scorching water over tealeaves. "Now I can't get you out from under my feet."

After a little thought I decided a reply of any kind wasn't required, not even a grunt, so watched Granny Bee click-clacking her knitting needles. I already knew what she was creating with those size twelves and a ball of bubblegum pink yarn. She'd taken to mass-producing tea cosies. Every single abode in Nickle Street was in possession of at least one of them.

"She did the same yesterday, an' all." Vera sniffed, fixed me with a narrow eyed stare.

I stared back. She looked a sorry state, thinner than ever, and heaven knows there wasn't enough meat on her bones before. Her roots were in dire need of a peroxide touch up. The coat of ivory pressed powder didn't quite do the job it was meant to do, didn't quite conceal her pale skin, the dark smudges beneath her peepers. That usual vodka enhanced glow, that flush that misled you into believing she was brimming with health, was missing. I should have dredged up a little pity for whatever misfortune had befallen her way. Instead the itch of impatience got to me first.

"So what?" I made sure my voice was practically dripping with sarcasm. "Crime now, is it, staying in?"

"Hear that, Joan?" Vera turned to Mum. "Hear how she talks to her elders?" She leaned east, jabbed a finger at my face. The nail was without its usual red lick of varnish. "Getting above your station, you are, young lady. Not too old for one of me famous Chinese burns, either." She straightened up, ran a shaky hand over her hair. "Full of the sauce lately, she is, Joan. Bloody disgraceful."

A fresh pot of tea was brought to the table, placed center, covered with a knitted cosy. From her extensive collection Mum had chosen the tulip red with narrow navy stripes.

"She's not the only one full of the sauce lately, is she, Vera?" she said.

I didn't even try to hide the smirk that stretched my lips. Ever since the encounter with Black Jack last Christmas Eve she'd gradually been upping her alcohol intake. Pretty soon Mum would be forced to take over her life, bed her down in the dossers room, keep her out of harm's way . It wouldn't be a walk in the park for any of us. You could bet your bottom dollar on it. There'd be no end of tears and tantrums from her. And then some more of the same from me. And even worse, in my opinion, was that over all those months she'd been viewing the world through the bottom of a bottle, she'd not once let slip any inside info I craved about Jack and herself and what went on in Soho with Uncle Stavros, R.I.P.

"Oh don't start, Joanie, not today." Vera snapped open her handbag, ferreted around in its depths, pulled out a pack of ten Woodbines, a box of matches. Obviously she was strapped for cash again. I knew that cos she only ever bought ten fags from Murphy's Corner Store when he refused her tick, was fed up with her not paying her dues.

"I know a secret," Granny Bee said.

We turned our attention towards Granny Bee. She laid her knitting upon her lap, crossed her arms, gave each of us a leisurely up and downer. We waited for her to continue.

Seconds passed. We waited longer. Mum splashed milk into cups, poured the brew through a tea strainer. Vera rubbed a fire stick along the edge of the matchbox. It flared, settled into a yellow flame. She held it to the tip of a Woodbine. The smell of sulphur stained the air. As for myself, well, the anticipation of hearing a secret first hand had me near on fit to bust.

Finally, Mum put me out of my misery. "What secret's that, Granny Bee?"

She tipped forward, tapped the side of her snozzle, said, "Too wayward for her own good, she is."

The breath I didn't even realise I'd been holding hissed from the lungs. As it was common knowledge we weren't the best of buddies, I suspected she was referring to me, put my guard in place ready to defend my good character against her verbal onslaught.

"That she is." Vera nodded agreement. "Been telling our Joanie the very same thing. I'm sorry to say this, Mrs. Bee, but your granddaughter needs reining in hard before she goes that far she can't find her way back."

I tutted, rolled my peepers three-sixty degrees. Granny Bee tutted, moved her knitting, patted her knee. Monty, the marmalade cat, took up residence on her lap, surveyed the scene. I challenged him to an eyeball to eyeball. He won again, buckled his legs, prepared himself to snooze for the rest of the afternoon.

"Not her, you idiot." Granny Bee hitched a thumb my way. I immediately took umbrage, threw her my best scowl, gave it extra weight with a growl.

"Well who then, if not her?" Mum hitched a thumb my way too.

I sighed. It seemed pretty clear I was a victim of persecution, so drew in breath, opened my mouth to bitterly complain, but before I could let those complaints off the leash Granny Bee interrupted.

"That girl from the Co-op, that's who," she said.

"What?" Vera said. "Do you mean Maureen with the tattooed boyfriend?"

I straightened my spine, flapped my lugholes. It wasn't often I got to be privy to a brand new piece of local titbit hot of the press. A couple of speculations sprung to mind.

One, the tattooed boyfriend had failed to take her to heaven and back so she'd sent him packing. Maureen was, after all's said and done, an enthusiastic women's libber, wouldn't put up with half measures, would she? And two, she'd gone and got herself in the pudding club, they'd be a rushed wedding, neighbours would nod and wink. Men would congratulate the tattooed boyfriend, women would silently commiserate with Maureen.

A rap on the back door cut through the speculating. It swung inwards. Old Ma Flowers wheezed her way into the kitchen.

"Ladies." Her fag husky voice sounded full of pleasurable anticipation. Her treble chins wobbled. She eased her well-padded carcass onto a chair. "Have you heard the latest?"

My concentration took a diversion, focused on Old Ma. Her ample derriere over- flowed the seat. Her heavy bosoms rested on the top roll of her belly. Mum fetched another cup, poured her a brew, said, "Not yet, but

I'm sure we're about to."

"Wait til you hear this." Old Ma Flowers chuckled, set the chins quivering. "You'll never believe it."

"For God's sake, Ma, just tell us then," Vera said, firing up another Woodbine. "Put an end to our suffering, why don't you."

Old Ma gave each of us a delighted smile, said, "Maureen from the Co-op has eloped."

There was a chorus of denials, a volley of questions, when, why, does her mother know?

"And what's more, ladies," Old Ma said, "she's not eloped with who you think she has, an' all."

"What?" Vera said. "Not with the tattooed boyfriend?"

"Nope. Not with him." Old Ma crossed her arms, let loose a loud guffaw closely followed by a fag induced coughing fit. "You'll never guess who it is, not in a million years, you won't."

It was about then I had a feeling of looming doom. The overwhelming urge to stop Old Ma talking was almost irresistible. I wanted to strangle the living daylights out of that woman, to clamp my fingers under her treble chins, squeeze until every last breath was gone from her body, cos the penny had finally dropped. I knew who Maureen's secret beau involved in the elopement was. And I didn't like it, not one little bit.

"It's that nice looking, long haired Polish boy from number twenty-three," Granny Bee said. "Him and her, going to San Francisco, they are."

All eyes lasered in on Granny Bee. A five seconds silence gave way to gasps, then the babble of four women talking over themselves disturbed the marmalade cat, woke me from a stunned stupor. Luckily I had the presence of mind to keep as quiet as a church mouse. It wasn't easy. Maureen from the Co-op had thieved my dream, thieved my one way ticket for a ride on the love train.

"How do you know who it is?" Old Ma flowers sounded most aggrieved. Her tone of voice was a clear indication.

"Well I'll tell you," Granny Bee said, "if I can get a word in edgeways, that it."

We gave her our full focus of attention. She stroked Monty, the marmalade cat, back to sleep, told us how she'd woken early that morning, cracked the foolproof lock on the front door, went to check the comings and goings in the street, just in case. Of course we all knew she was really out there just in hope, just in hope the Greek sailor showed. So she'd taken a sit on the red chair beside the gate.

"Oh it was lovely out there." She sighed. "Peaceful, wasn't even sunrise yet."

"And then what?" Vera said.

"And then the girl from the Co-op comes along lugging a suitcase and stops at number twenty-three," Granny Bee said, " and that nice looking boy gets out of that painted wagon of his and they kiss. Oh it were ever so romantic, ladies, and then they saw me."

She fell silent, took a trip to that other world she's apt to visit on a regular basis. I took the opportunity to put two and two together. Maybe all wasn't lost. Maybe it wasn't the disaster I feared it was. Maybe Nick the Hippie was doing Maureen from the Co-op a favour, giving her an early dawn morning lift to the train station, or the bus depot, helping her escape the stifling attentions of the overzealous tattooed boyfriend. And the matter of the kiss. Well, didn't have to mean anything, did it? After all, it was the summer of love, there was a lot of meaningless kisses happening, a lot of meaningless pecks here, there and everywhere. We were spreading the love.

"And then what?" Vera said.

"So I asks what's going on, don't I?" Granny Bee said, "And the nice looking boy crosses the street, tells me it's a secret, they're off to Amerikey, joining a wagon train, of all things. Bloody fools, everyone knows that place is full of injuns, don't they? Anyways," she treated Old Ma to a sniff and a hard look, "their secret was safe with me til Old Ma Blabbermouth turns up and spills the beans."

I carefully slid the chair back, slowly rose, prayed the hammering of my heart wasn't that loud, didn't alert the others to my presence , didn't prompt Mum to look at me too closely, to see that something was terribly amiss, cos she knew things about me before I even knew them myself. Luckily the tea and talk brigade was in full speculation swing. I made it undetected through the back door, down the side alley, out onto the pavement. The passion wagon was missing. Only a dark slick of leaked engine oil was left behind. And me, of course. And my broken dreams.

I heard the pad of footsteps, turned my head east. Frankie Doyle was walking towards me. I gave him the once over, bottom to top, baseball boots, black, white laces, jeans, dark denim, navy coloured jumper. As usual the guitar accompanied him, slung across his shoulder. I wondered how awkward this first face to face after the dirty deed was likely to be. He stopped half a dozen steps away. We sized each other up. He nodded towards number twenty-three. Our peepers followed the direction of his nod.

"Guess you've heard the latest then," he said, "about the hippie and Maureen?"

"Yep," I said.

"Haven't seen you around for a couple of days," he said. "What you been up to?"

"Oh you know." I made my tone light and breezy. "Not much."

"Yeah, me neither." He shuffled the baseball boots. "Ruby?"

"Yes?" I took a quick glance at him, read the questions hanging on the tip of his tongue I didn't have the answers to, prayed he wouldn't ask them. I must have prayed hard enough.

"Doesn't matter," he said, "it's nothing important," and he swung open the gate, paced along the garden path, disappeared through the front door.

I took a deep breath, let it slowly out. I wasn't proud of myself for brushing him off, for hurting his feelings. For a split second a wave of regret took me by surprise. Frankie Doyle was such a safe bet. I'd be sitting comfy until death do us part with him. The faint sound of a tune came drifting from a couple of doors down. I gave a wry smile. Mr. McCartney was inviting me to join Sgt. Pepper's Lonely Hearts Club Band. I was the ideal candidate.

24

There were a number of reasons why I packed a rucksack and took off for Soho, and all of them were legit. I followed my Dad's advice, travelled light like an old soldier, couple of basics and a toothbrush. The plan was to steal away at dead of night when only tom cats and no-gooders were on the make, catch the earliest London bound train, then the tube, maybe to Oxford Circus or Piccadilly, then put some wear on the soles of my shoes the rest of the way to the Hive, wait for Big Shirley to emerge, surprise, surprise, guess who's turned up for a visit. Obviously she wouldn't be overly delighted, but what could she do about it once she'd heard my tale of woe? After all, she'd played a leading role in that whole sorry state of affairs, hadn't she?

Anyway, back to the reasons that caused me to quickstep it to the city of bright lights.

Needless to say it all began to go wrong when Black Jack made his presence known at nearly midnight on New Year's Eve. He brought a gun for company and a backup warning, something about Uncle Stavros messing with the big boys, and before Dad could shake a leg, a slug of lead had personally escorted my Uncle to the pearly gates to meet his maker. And Granny Bee moved herself and Monty, the marmalade cat, in with us. Both made my life a misery. And then knocked up Strawberry Blonde Stella darkened our doorstep, then done a flit, left the baby behind with her dirty washing. Turns out her and my Uncle had indulged in a little slap and tickle with dire consequences. And all the while I'd been coping with an unhealthy love interest in Denny Doyle, and the foolhardiness of living on Nick the Hippy's dreams, and then, brave on the doctored fruit punch at the fancy dress party, I'd given Frankie, who I knew darn well liked me more than I liked him, I gave him the green light to show me what fits where. And the constant drip drip of Granny Bee losing more and more of her marbles down the back alley of the past just tipped me over the edge. I've lost count of the number of times I've prayed for God to take her into his fold without a moments delay.

Unfortunately, it wasn't a prayer he felt willing to grant. But he very kindly delivered Vera into the shambles as compensation. As if things weren't bad enough already, they were about to get a whole lot worse. Vodka Vera came a cropper. It was the last straw.

She turned up late for Dad's famous Sunday morning fry up. I knew it was serious cos she'd brought with her the faded rose-coloured vanity case, the case that held all her important papers. I sneaked a sideways look at her, wondered if she was broken beyond repair this time. She sat, placed the case at her feet, kept her peepers from landing on ours. It was safe to suppose that the blues had a firm grip on her once again, that she was in the limbo of hell.

Without a single word of exchange, Dad slid a plate of bacon, sausage, fried bread and two eggs sunny side up in front of her. Mum stood, poured a brew, walked around the kitchen table, set the steaming beverage alongside. She dropped her left palm upon Vera's shoulder, gave a pat, a squeeze, returned to her place. Baby Andreas whimpered. Granny Bee fed a bacon titbit to Monty the marmalade cat. I let my peepers travel from face to face, then settled them back on Granny Bee. She'd taken to staring at Vera's bowed head. I wondered if she was verging on one of her rare lucid moments, wondered if a tasty shred of a past scandal would be forthcoming. I was in luck.

"When are you going to stop killing yourself with guilt, Vera Williams?" she said.

I pretended to be interested in nothing bar the half eaten fry-up, hoped nobody noticed the air of crackling anticipation that was surely flashing like bolts of lightning around me.

"Duchess." Dad's voice had the ring of a warning to it. I heard it loud and clear. Fortunately, Granny Bee didn't.

"Well, for heaven's sake, it's more than twenty years ago now, Vera," Granny Bee said. "Don't you think you've paid your dues at least twice over already?"

From undercover of my fringe I discreetly took a butcher's at Vera. More luck was shining down on me that day. Through her vodka glazed eyes that old British bulldog fighting spirit I'd heard reminisced about a thousand times gave a little flare. The champion mud wrestler of '44 was still alive and kicking.

"Duchess!" This time Dad's tone was that sharp it could have easily sliced the tongue clean out of your mouth. I noticed Mum laid a hand upon

Granny Bee's arm. They'd gone for the double silencer attack. I wondered if that was the end of the promising spat, wondered if she'd take the hint, wondered if I'd ever learn the truth of why Vera Williams was killing herself with guilt. Much to my delight Granny Bee executed a nifty duck and swerve, outmanoeuvred the opposition under the disguise of being a genuine nutcase.

"Well, call yourself a true East Ender, do you, Vera?" Granny Bee's voice practically dripped with venom. "Huh! Try pulling the other one, it's got bells on."

With a trembling hand Vera picked up her cup, took a sip of tea. The rattle of china against china rang out as she settled it back upon the saucer. She straightened her spine, squared her shoulders.

"I am a true East Ender." There was a note of pride along with the slight vodka slur. "Born within the sound of Bow bells, I was."

"Well, no East Ender I ever knew rolled over like a licked dog." Granny Bee sniffed, crossed her arms. "You best clean your bloody act up, do us all a favour."

"So what does a West End old fool like you know about anything?" Vera jabbed a forefinger at Granny Bee. "You wants to keep your sticky beak out of other people's business, you do."

I can assure you I was brimming with glee at that precise moment. The spilling of beans was shaping up very nicely. Everyone knows when tempers get lost in the heat of the moment things are said, things that wouldn't normally be said, things like secrets. Whatever happened more than twenty years ago which was killing Vera with guilt would soon reach my lugholes. It was a God given. I smiled encouragingly at Granny Bee. After all, it was her turn to add to the verbal fisticuffs, wasn't it. She opened her mouth. I held my breath.

"Ladies!" Dad interrupted. "I'm warning you both; don't go starting up with that bloody East and West bickering. I'm in no mood for your shenanigans this morning."

The breath rushed out of my airbags taking all likelihood of earwigging on a secret with it. I treated Dad to my best disgusted look. He raised an eyebrow, gave me his best uninterested look.

"Now you just hold your horses a minute, Michael George Blackbee." Granny Bee held up a hand. "I've got one more thing to say." I re-focused on her. A quiver of hope rolled my belly over. "What about those bloody towers?"

A drawn-out groan escaped my lips. I couldn't believe that at such a crucial point in my earwigging history Granny Bee's mind had up and left and gone for a Burton. I pushed the remains of my fry-up away.

"What bloody towers?" I said.

"Nothing but a cheap fix, them," Vera said. "Ripping the heart and soul out of the place, they are."

"That they are." Granny Bee nodded agreement. "Nowt but a breeding ground for rats and rogues."

I sighed. Any chance of hearing why Vera was killing herself with guilt was lost in the fog of Granny Bee's memory. On the radio Eric began to tell his girl about a dirty old part of the city where the sun refused to shine. He reckoned they had to get out of that place even if it's the last thing they ever do. And that's exactly what I ought to do too. I didn't fit in here. I didn't belong around this neck of the woods. I never had.

"Will you stop your daydreaming, Ruby, and go help Dad set up the spare room."

I scraped my chair back, set off for the dossers room with a heavy step.

"And you can stop stamping your feet an' all," Mum added.

"She's a handful, that girl, Joanie," Vera said.

"Too much like her father, that's the trouble," Granny Bee said.

Under my breath I grumbled about being nothing but a general dogsbody and gofer. I also added a bit about child slavery being abolished. And just for good measure, once I was certain they were out of earshot, I told them all to bugger off. By the time I reached the front room I was far from feeling in a sunny disposition. Dad eyed me over.

"So," he said, "they sent you, did they, our little ray of goodness and light?"

I curled my lip Elvis style, rolled my peepers. When they stopped rolling I set them on Dad's face with a cool glare. He had no trouble matching the cool glare with one of his own. We stood that way until he held out the olive branch.

"Okay, I give in," he said. "What're you in a two and eight about this time, Ruby?"

I took a few seconds to get my thoughts together, decided slowly slowly would probably give me better results. Nobody likes to be interrogated, do they? Nobody likes the truth stretched out of them on the old emotional rack. I had to be canny, had to choose my words carefully. But I wasn't skilled at talking people into a false sense of security. And I wasn't confident Dad would appreciate it. He had a low tolerance for any kind of waffling.

"Come on then, spit it out," Dad said. "As much as I enjoy your wonderful company, there is this beast of a sofa bed to do battle with, you know."

"Promise to tell the truth, then?" I said.

"I always tell the truth, me darlin'."

"Cross your heart and hope to die?"

"Stick a needle in my eye," Dad said.

"Why is Vera killing herself with guilt?"

The question hanged between us for an eternity. I kept my peepers firmly fastened on his, watched for any tell-tell sign of anything I could use to pull his answer apart, 'cos I was darned sure he wouldn't willingly give me the truth, the whole truth and nothing but the truth.

"Oh, I see," he said. "Have you ever thought that if she wanted you to know her business she'd have told you herself?"

"Nobody tells me anything," I said. "Everybody else knows everything except me. This family's full of the hush-hush where I'm concerned. We've more skeletons in our closet than the bloody graveyard."

"Poor you." There was a slight hint of sarcasm about his voice. I thought it wise to ignore it, continued to press home the unfairness of keeping secrets in the dark.

"I have a right to know," I said.

"Oh do you indeed?" At that point it did cross my mind that I may have just scuppered the chances of learning more. Dad also had a low tolerance about me demanding my rights, any rights, actually, and especially my rights about staying out til midnight.

"I just want to know, Dad." I sighed, perched on the arm of the sofa bed, waited whilst he put together a gasper, whilst he decided whether to indulge my want to know or not.

"Well, Ruby, the truth of the matter is she lost her family in the London blitz," Dad said. "She hasn't coped since, took to the bottle to drown her sorrows. Bloody dirty rotten shame, it is, and now the demon drink has her in its grip, and probably always will til she finally curls her toes up."

I wasted a minute digesting the explanation. It seemed perfectly feasible, although my gut instinct told me there was more than that to it, a lot more than that. For starters, somewhere along the line, Black Jack was involved in the downfall of Vera Williams. What part did he play in that well-guarded secret? And where was he now? What was he doing? Why hadn't the cops got him for my Uncle Stavros' murder? Cos I was as sure as the sun rises in the east he had a hand in that too.

"And that's it, is it, that's all of it, the whole kit and caboodle?" I said.

"Why, isn't that enough of a reason for you then?" Dad said. "Isn't that enough to make anyone tread the rocky road to ruin? What more do you want, me Dixie darlin'?"

We stared at each other for the longest time. He knew I knew there was more to tell. Same as he knew I knew he'd silenced me into a corner. But as far as I was concerned it wasn't done with yet. One day I would hear Vera Williams' secrets, would hear all there was to hear. But before that happened, I had to take Eric's advice and get out of this place.

25

Whilst waiting for the perfect time to spring into action I packed my rucksack. I was travelling light like an old soldier, a toothbrush and a few rags. Then I put together a letter, addressed it to Dad. There wasn't much to write. Then I listened to the sounds of the world preparing to sleep, unless you were a tomcat or no gooder, of course. They'd be preparing themselves for something altogether different. They'd be slipping through the night hours on the lookout for golden opportunities, wouldn't they?

The old grandmother clock downstairs informed me it was midnight. Dead on cue I heard Granny Bee open the bedroom window, call in Monty, the marmalade cat. He took his own sweet time before answering the call, before the thud of his paws on the dustbin lid, then the tin roof of the outside lavvy, announced his return. I gave her ten minutes to tuck herself in before parting the curtains. I peered outside. It was a beautiful August night.

The white half-moon gave the world a pale glow. Stars winked off and on. I saw silhouettes of the houses beyond the piece of scrub land. One by one their yellow stained panes of glass turned black as folk inside hit the sack, drifted away to the land of nod. I opened my window, leaned out a little, breathed in the scent of late flowering blooms. Movement from the garden next door caught my attention. Steven Shaw was patrolling the chain-link fencing. He'd travelled back to the Far East. At least in his mind he had. Occasionally he ducked down, made himself small. Maybe a noise reminded him of something too unspeakable for words, maybe gunfire, maybe the screams of tortured souls, maybe the killing of his friend Sonny Jim. The back door opened. In a wedge of lemon light stood Philip Shaw. Once again he'd come to fetch his brother home, back home from the demons of war that tormented him still.

The night sky darkened. The moon and stars shone brighter. I heard the high-pitched yips of a fox. There was no return call. I saw the form of a cat, belly low, slink across the recently mown lawn. The clock downstairs struck three. One more hour then I'd be for the off. I was in for a long walk. The green double-decker wouldn't be in service yet, but if my calculations were correct I'd ride the first ferry across the narrow stretch of murky water, catch the first London-bound train from Pompey Hard.

The need to sleep began to whine. I struggled to stop the blinkers from dropping down south. The bed was practically begging for me to keep it company. I really needed to stay alert, have my faculties about me. Everybody knows that tiredness messes with clear thinking, don't they? I've heard enough stories about P.O.Ws being so sleep-deprived they didn't know which way was up. Then I had a brainwave, decided to sit the last hour out in the kitchen. Those hard chairs aren't built for comfort. There was no chance of snuggling in perched on one of those. Unfortunately, it proved to be a fatal mistake.

I let one eye take a look round the bedroom door. On the landing sixty watts blazed as always 'cos I still wasn't a fan of the dark. Good news though. All other doors were shut tight. I exercised the precaution of listening for a minute or two longer, heard the muted tick-tock of the grandmother clock, the muffled snores of Granny Bee, the groans of a house at rest. I made a move, dodged the creaky stair, stepped over the squeaky hall floorboard, tip-toed into the kitchen. It was gloomy. My peepers needed a moment to adjust, then they picked out the shape of a dresser inherited from an Aunt Mimi I never knew, the shape of the gas cooker with eye level grill, the shape of a body sitting at the table. My heart missed a beat, restarted at double quick time.

"Take a seat, Dixie darlin', think a little chat's in order, don't you?"

The breath I'd been holding escaped, made a soft hiss through my teeth. I heard the grind of the Zippos' wheel against flint, smelled the aroma of lighter fuel, saw the flare of fire touch the Sun Valley roll-up.

"Well come on then, Ruby, look lively, haven't got all day to waste waiting on you."

"You nearly gave me a heart attack, Dad." I slipped the rucksack off my shoulder, dropped it on the red quarry tiles, took up Mum's battle stance. "What are you doing down here anyways?"

"More like what are you doing creeping around in the small wee hours?"

Dad often answered a question with a question of his own. It was a favourite interrogation tactic of his, one that always broke my steely reserve not to buckle under pressure. I parked myself at the table, made a show of being hard done by.

"Truth is, Dad," I said, "for my own sake; I've got to get away from this place."

"I see." He stalled a while, rubbed a calloused hand over chin stubble, heaved himself upright, took two steps to the dresser, fiddled with the radio, found a pirate station broadcasting from a rusty old ship bobbing about on the briny. Long John Baldry encouraged his listeners to let the heartaches begin. Little did he know mine had already begun some time ago.

"And if you stop me today I'm only going to try again tomorrow," I said. "So it's best you save us all the bother of waiting for the inevitable, isn't it?"

"Well, well," Dad said, "that's quite a statement. What's brought you to this plan of action, Dixie darlin'? Boy trouble?"

"Partly." I sighed, placed elbows on the table top, cupped my chin between palms.

"You do know, Ruby, don't you," Dad matched my sigh, "that whoever this boy is, he most definitely won't be your first or last Romeo?"

"It's not just about boys, Dad, it's everything."

"Everything?" Dad said. "Poor you, life must be hell."

I could hear the sarcasm dripping, so hummed a growl at him, the low pitched growl I use when feeling unfairly judged. Then I threw the classic one liner his way, made sure it was heavy on the side of accusation.

"I knew you wouldn't understand."

Silence stretched. The crackle of Rizla blue burning seemed loud. The old station platform clock ticked away the seconds.

"Oh I understand perfectly." Dad said. "I know you want to be someplace else. Been wanting that for quite a while, haven't you?"

"I just don't want what's expected of me, Dad."

In my mind I clearly saw what was expected of me. Leave school, find a dead-end job, maybe in a factory, maybe a shop, until I got hitched, maybe to second choice Frankie, followed by babies, cooking, cleaning, idle gossip, evenings in front the telly, growing old before I'd even had a chance to live. I didn't want that life. I didn't want to wake up and suddenly find my best days were behind me.

"Nor did I, Ruby," Dad said, "nor did I. But running away isn't the answer. It never is."

"Well, your army buddy Black Jack thought it was the perfect answer, didn't he?" The words escaped from my mouth before the brain knew what was what. And every single one was laced with pure poison. "And got away with murder, he did, didn't he?"

Dad took a long drag on the roll-up. In the half light I watched his grey eyes narrow, harden like slithers of flint. Many a fool's been felled at twenty paces by a single stare from my Dad. I wondered if I'd taken a step too far, finally pushed his patience to the limit. I wondered if he knew how much I regretted being cursed with a temper I wasn't yet in control of. I wondered if he knew I loved him. I'd never told him. We weren't the kind of family given to sentimental confessions of the heart.

"Jack never runs away," Dad said, "not from anyone or anything."

With great effort I kept my peepers on his. I'm not sure what I actually saw in those dark depths, but whatever it was I didn't feel overly keen to pay it a visit. Even so, I couldn't resist stepping a little closer to the edge.

"Then why are you looking for him?" I said. "Tell the truth, Dad."

"I always tell the truth." He pressed his spine against the back of the chair. "If I believe it's really wanted, or needed."

"Well I really want it, Dad." I too leaned back, crossed my arms. "I really, really want to hear the truth, the whole truth and nothing less. Why are you looking for Black Jack?"

"To stop him looking for revenge."

I gave myself the luxury of a few minutes to digest the information. Revenge? For what? It was Black Jack who packed a gun. I recalled last Christmas Eve, time waltzing towards midnight, him on our doorstep, acting crazy, waving that piece of army issue metal, talking in riddles, talking about Uncle Stavros messing with the big boys. And then I began putting two and two together. And, even though I knew the answer wouldn't be what I wanted to hear, I couldn't help asking anyways.

"It was the big boys, wasn't it, Dad? They did for my Uncle Stavros, didn't they? Tell me the truth, Dad, tell me it was them."

I watched him fix a roll-up, watched him place it between his lips, watched the Zippos' flame turn from blue to yellow. He blew a smoke ring. I watched it float north, disappear into thin air. Then I waited for him to confirm how right I was. Instead he confirmed I couldn't have been more wrong.

"The big boys put the squeeze on," Dad said. "But your Uncle squeezed the trigger himself."

I hadn't known until then that silence could be so painfully loud. The clock ticked. Every second boomed like a shot from a cannon. Outside the dawn chorus was awakening. Musical notes tripped over musical notes, a full orchestra tuning up. The blood rushed through my veins, deafening, like a wild sea crashing onto the shore. Even the breath I breathed was a harsh grating sound in my ears. And yet my cry of denial sounded weak, a pathetic mew in the stillness of an early morning when only the milkie should be up and doing his rounds.

"Yes," Dad said, "that's exactly what he did, Ruby. And now you know. The truth doesn't always sit easy, me darlin'. Sometimes it leaves more questions than there are answers to."

Well, I can tell you he was spot on about that. Even more questions ran through my thoughts faster than a snippet of gossip spreads through the neighbourhood, tumbling over one another, jostling for my attention. Where to start? Who should I start with? Guess it had to be Uncle Stavros, didn't it? What was he doing messing with the big boys? Why would they put the squeeze on him? What could be so bad he'd play Russian roulette with his life, with all our lives? And what about Granny Bee's Greek sailor? Did he really end up in the swanee wearing a pair of concrete boots? And then there was Vodka Vera. Why was she drinking herself into the grave on the nectar of Smirnoff? Or the cheap equivalent if she were brassic. And where did Black Jack fit into her treading the rocky road to ruin? 'Cos he did fit into it somewhere along the line. He was tied up in it all right. But how? Dad interrupted my dilemma.

"If you're going, Ruby, you best get going now."

The idea of staying put suddenly seemed very favourable. After all, the familiar brought its own comforts, didn't it? For starters I knew everybody, and everybody knew me. I knew the streets, the back alleys, the short cuts. I knew what was expected. Perhaps it wouldn't be that bad. I hesitated, took a moment to weigh up my options. And then that old troublemaker called fate stepped in. On the radio Ray Davies reckoned he was in paradise gazing on a Waterloo sunset. Well, that must surely be some sight to see, mustn't it? And I wanted to see it. I picked up the rucksack, made for the back door, slid the bolts across.

"Big Shirley's expecting you," Dad said.

I closed my peepers, took a deep breath. I felt the heat of anger rise to boiling point in five seconds flat. I did my best to damp it down. It wasn't easy, not when it seemed I couldn't even do a flit without it being general knowledge. The blinkers rolled up. I stared at the wire-meshed pane of glass in the door, gathered my dignity, decided on one more interrogation before I bid adios and good riddance to bad rubbish. I turned. The kitchen was empty. Dad had already gone.

26

I set off along Nickle Street at a brisk pace. I was running late, thanks to that unsettling encounter with Dad, was still somewhat irked he hadn't even said good-bye, or begged me to reconsider. I thought at the very least he'd put his foot down, forbid me to leave the house, threaten me with that good hiding I've never had in all my fifteen and three-quarter years. But no, he let me swan off without as much as a how do you do. My feelings were hurt, my mood far from rosy. That's probably why I didn't bother hiding my annoyance when a familiar voice said, "Oi oi, saveloy, want a lift?"

I slapped the brakes on my shoes, tilted my chin east. Second-hand Sid eased his car to a smooth halt. I gave him my best icy glare. He failed to pick up on it, gave his usual friendly smile, the smile that made it difficult to stay annoyed. I still tried my hardest though, took two steps forward, leaned my face through the open front passenger window. I noticed the trademark cheroot nestled in the left hand corner of his mouth, smelled the slightly sweet aroma when he indulged in a drag.

"You know what, Mr Sid?" For his benefit I used my finest patronising voice. "I very much doubt you're going my way, actually, so thanks, but no thanks."

I waited for Mr Sid to respond. My disposition was ripe for a little verbal discharge. He would be the perfect target. He didn't disappoint.

"How do you know I'm not going your way?" he said. "You a bloody clairvoyant now, are you?"

It was then I made the second fatal mistake of the day. And it wasn't even breakfast time yet. I straightened up, said, "Because, Mr Sid," and I heard the firm conviction of my words, "I'm going to London, Soho, to be precise. Hardly your neck of the woods, is it?"

And that's when Second-hand Sid made his fatal mistake.

"Well, ain't that some coincidence. Must be your lucky day." I heard the faint accent he had from somewhere I couldn't place. "Just so happens I'm picking up a couple of top nobs from around that way. Jump in, Ruby, save you the cost of a train fare."

He tilted across, pushed the car door open. We stared at one another. I silently picked apart his fatal mistake, 'cos it surely was a fatal mistake, 'cos he should have asked if my parents knew I was taking off to the city of bright lights, if I had their approval, or their permission even. And not only that, he wasn't dressed for picking up a couple of top nobs from anywhere, didn't have his chauffeur's glad rags on, the black suit, white shirt, peaked cap. And another dead giveaway, the car was no sleek luxury limo, just a tidy run of the mill saloon. I smelled a rat.

"Well, what d'ya say, Ruby? Want a lift or not?" He drummed the fingers of his right hand on the steering wheel. "Makes no odds to me."

For a number of seconds I wrestled with making a decision. On the one hand it still rankled that too many people knew I was going on the run. On the other hand it seemed petty to refuse such a generous offer. I slid onto the front passenger seat, hugged my rucksack against my chest, stared straight ahead through the windscreen. I didn't feel inclined to engage in the small talk. Unfortunately Second-hand Sid did.

"So," he said, "got any plans once you hit Soho? Got somewhere to stay?"

"Mr Sid." I threw him a sigh heavy on the haughty side. "Everything's taken care of."

"So you've a roof over your head and a job then?" he said. "Going to need money to survive, aren't you? Nothing's free, is it, except for bad luck, eh?"

Of course I hadn't taken the matter of money into consideration. After all, I was only a teenager with all the many problems that entailed. Nobody my age worried about the cost of living. We were famous for being delusional young mercenaries, weren't we? And lest we dared to forget, our parents mentioned it on a regular basis, that the younger generation had never had it so good. And I'll tell you something for nothing, pretty soon I'd learn they were telling the truth, pretty soon my rose-tinted glasses would be shattered beyond repair. In the meantime, though, I wasn't about to admit to Second-hand Sid he'd found a flaw in my best laid plan, decided on evasive tactics instead.

"You weren't really going to London, were you, Mr Sid?" I said.

"No," he said, "I was just going nowhere."

My interest in other people's business was immediately alerted. I wondered if his fair maiden Marjory Watkins knew he was cruising the streets just going nowhere. I wondered if he was perhaps doing a little racketeering as a side line. I wondered what it was about Second-hand Sid that made him ever so slightly different. And then I wondered how to get the conversation juices flowing, decided on a sure-fire bet. The war.

"I was wondering, Mr Sid," I said. "What did you do in the war?"

"The war?"

His voice was soft; I barely heard it, tipped my chin rightwards, noticed the tension in his jaw, caught a flash of anguish darken his eyes before he pulled himself together. I had an uneasy feeling I wouldn't ever be the same if I heard his war story. Maybe a bit of back- pedalling would be best for both our sakes.

"I was only wondering." I hitched a shoulder, let it drop. "You don't have to tell me."

"The war." He didn't take the hint, took a shaky breath. "I spent the war running and running til there was no where left to run to. And then I was just a number."

I don't mind admitting my curiosity was spurred into action. Why was he running? Or what was he running from? Maybe he was an evacuee and absconded. Or maybe he got the call up papers and went AWOL. Maybe that's when he got a number, when he enlisted to fight for Queen and country. My Dad could still recite his army number at the drop of a hat. I wondered if he and Mum were missing me yet.

"What do you mean, Mr Sid?" I said.

"Where I come from, Ruby," he said, "was not a good place for Jews, gypsies and poor unfortunates."

"Where do you come from then, Mr Sid?" I turned east in the seat, took a look at his profile, noted the signs of old age creeping up, deep lines on his face, jowls beginning to sag, black hair smattered with grey. "And what's Jews, gypsies and poor unfortunates got to do with you?"

"I'm a Jew, Ruby, from Amsterdam. You'll not read of my war in any history books. See this?" He pushed his shirt sleeve up, stretched his left arm west. "They tattooed a number on my skin so I'll never forget. Oy oy oy, as if I ever could, huh? I'm the sole survivor from my family, everyone else, all dead, everyone else just a memory."

"All dead, Mr Sid?" My voice held a tone of disbelief about it.

"Yes, all dead, my mother, my papa, my little sisters, aunts, uncles, cousins, all dead."

He briefed me scanty details, details about segregation, persecution, annihilation. I stared at the faint greyish blue numbers, ran my right index finger across them. They were smooth to the touch. I didn't understand. Who cared where you came from, or what faith you were? After all, you couldn't be more popular round my way than Antonio the Eyetaliano, the famous ice-cream seller. And even though Mr O'Connor from up the road complained about the boisterous merry making at Christmas, nobody minded he was a JW, did they? And then there was Jeremy Baker. It didn't bother us one iota he preferred to dress in the spirit of Monroe. But we were the anti-war generation, weren't we? We were into spreading the love, smelling the roses, banning the bomb. Why, hadn't Mr McGuire warned us we were on the eve of destruction if we didn't change our ways and soon?

"But enough dwelling on the past," Mr Sid said. "I'll sing you a song, a celebration song, in my old language."

I rolled my peepers three-sixty degrees. He tapped out a beat with his left hand on the steering wheel. I waited for him to begin. Whilst waiting I piled up a million questions I felt duty bound to ask, all the whys, whats and wherefores. But I never did ask a single one. Mr Sid sang, strange guttural words, hava nagila, hava nagila. And when he was done I saw him brush away a tear. We travelled in silence for the remainder of the journey. The dead weight of history travelled with us.

"We're here," Second-hand Sid said.

I took a look around. There was The Bee Hive in all its tacky glory. The boards were removed from its sashed windows. I wondered why. Maybe Dad had relented, let the club re-open. Maybe he didn't know. I admired the stained glass, the double doors advertising its wares, ales, fine wines, spirits. I thought fine wines was probably stretching the truth, thought cheap plonk from the Cash and Carry more likely.

To the west Pot-Belly Stan came out the door of The Greasy Spoon. The smell of bacon cooking came out with him. He stared across the street at us in the tidy saloon. I stared back, added a sneer for extra effect. In return his mouth made a wry smile. A couple of men squeezed past him, disappeared into the cafe. Considering the early hour, I guessed they were heading for the docklands, to graft away eight hours for a weekly buff coloured wage packet full of the readies. Or perhaps they were barrow boys in need of a full English before spending the day bantering with their buyers.

I heard the faint strains of music, cocked a lughole. Steve Marriott was telling about his escapades at Itchycoo Park. Apparently, if you cross over the bridge of sighs, pass under dreaming spires, you'll find the park at Little Ilford. Apparently, it's all too beautiful there. I made a mental note to pay it a visit, see for myself what the attraction was about.

A young woman came teetering in dangerous heels along the middle of the street, brunette hair messy, blue coat hanging open, tangerine orange shift dress beneath. I decided she was out and about for one of two reasons. First, she was late for work, had no time to smarten up. Second, she was last to leave a pub lock-in. By the state of her I'd bet my bottom dollar on the second scenario.

"You want a lift home, Ruby? It's okay to change your mind, you know."

Second-hand Sid nudged my thoughts back to the here and now. How easy it would be to sit tight, to go home, back home to the familiar, back to the safety of a life I knew. I don't mind admitting I was tempted. But in my heart of hearts I was sure it wasn't what I really wanted. And anyways, I was there already, wasn't I?

"I'm here now," I said, "may as well see if this is where I'm meant to be, hadn't I?"

"May as well," Second-hand Sid said. "Sometimes you need to roam a little before you find where you best fit in."

I turned towards him, gave him a long look. He did likewise.

"I'm glad you roamed my way, Mr Sid." I placed my hand over the faint greyish blue numbers on his left forearm. "You're probably the nicest man I'll ever meet."

He laughed, slipped a small card from his wallet, said, "Take this, Ruby, my business card, phone number's on it, call if you need a lift going nowhere again."

I tucked the card into my rucksack, opened the car door, heaved myself out, watched Second-hand Sid turn left at the junction, disappear from sight, Then I watched Jesus stroll along the pavement, black hair still brushing the collar of his greatcoat. So, he'd been resurrected once more, been welcomed back into the fold, the man I'd truly believed was a good for nothing murdering son of a gun. He stopped at The Greasy Spoon. I kept my peepers firmly on him. He kept his on me. We stayed that way for longer than was comfy.

His mouth tried on a smile. I let mine do the same. I guessed a truce was called on the misunderstanding. I wondered if he'd be a soft touch for the stories, wondered if he'd be willing to tell me his role in Vodka Vera's rocky road to ruin, 'cos he played a role all right, a major role, that much I knew for sure. It took the dulcet tones of a forty fags a day Scouse drag queen to break us apart.

"Well, will you look who it ain't, the bloody squirt, no less. Still short, I see."

My attention swung to the first floor of The Bee Hive. For a moment I almost believed the vision of Marlene Dietrich was hanging out the window, half expected her to declare herself falling in love again. And I saw something too, I saw that her hospitality towards me was still on the thin side. I treated her to a wide smile, with teeth on show for added measure.

"Best let me in then, Big Shirley," I said. "You've got yourself a Blackbee back in residence."

The window slammed shut. I heard Pot-Belly Stan give a chuckle, heard him say, "Just like old times, eh, Jack?"

The front door opened. Big Shirley appeared. I gave her an up-and-downer, took in the silk pyjamas in a shocking shade of cerise, the red feather boa, green sequinned slippers. It shouldn't have worked. Somehow, on her, it just did. She threw a few poses. I crossed the street, gave her another up-and-downer, a sneer, a curl of the lip.

"So, what do you think?" She performed a couple of twirls. "Like it?"

"Ever heard of colour co-ordination, Shirley?" I said.

"No style, that's your trouble, squirt," she said. "Not many could carry off this combination and get away with it, you know."

"Not many would want to." I made sure my tone was generously flavoured with scorn, shouldered past her into the square hall. Everything was exactly the same as the last time I stood there, the chequered black and white floor, the sideboard with mother of pearl inlay, maybe from some far-flung land, maybe India. On the left the stairs climbed the wall to the first floor. On the right the heavy duty door leading into the bar.

"So," Big Shirley began climbing the stairs, "how long you staying for?"

"As long as I want to," I said.

"In that case you best learn some house rules, and learn them fast." Big Shirley sniffed. "By the way, were you ever told about the time the Krays tried to muscle in around here? "

"No, I wasn't." I kept my voice edged with boredom, didn't want to seem too keen, or run the risk of Big Shirley suddenly becoming struck dumb. But I can assure you, beneath my ribcage, my heart had broken into a quickstep. My thirst for other people's business was about to be quenched. I could hardly wait.

"Oh my gawd, squirt, that was one hell of a rum do, I can tell you. If it wasn't for your father and Jack …"

But then I stopped listening. Out of the corner of my right peeper I noticed something amiss, pulled my feet to a halt. Big Shirley continued on up. I reversed three stairs down.

The heavy duty door leading into the bar stood ajar. And I swear, as God's my witness, I heard Sinatra singing. I heard him singing about the summer wind blowing in. Like he did once before.

The End.

Lightning Source UK Ltd.
Milton Keynes UK
UKHW020651070223
416609UK00012B/2806